D1585419

Where Guns Talk

Ahead was a cold-blooded killer and an innocent woman who wanted to believe he was no such thing. Behind was a God-fearing tyrant by the name of Isaac Madie and Madie's three sons, all of them with vengeance in mind.

And Blake Durant was caught smack in the middle.

He wanted to rescue the woman and return a fortune in gold bullion to its rightful owners. But Madie had other ideas. And if it came to that, so did Ringo Nyall, the killer who'd set his mind on the gold … and the girl!

Where Guns Talk

Sheldon B. Cole

A Black Horse Western

ROBERT HALE

First published by Cleveland Publishing Co. Pty Ltd,
New South Wales, Australia
First published in 1967
© 2020 Mike Stotter and David Whitehead

This edition © The Crowood Press, 2020

ISBN 978-0-7198-3126-3

The Crowood Press
The Stable Block
Crowood Lane
Ramsbury
Marlborough
Wiltshire SN8 2HR

www.bhwesterns.com

Robert Hale is an imprint
of The Crowood Press

Typeset by Simon and Sons ITES Services Pvt Ltd
Printed and bound in Great Britain by
4Bind Ltd, Stevenage, SG1 2XT

ONE

BUILT FOR DISTANCE

The dry westerly came hot off the plains. Blake Durant turned his black stallion, Sundown, out of the wind's blast and looked at the town below the butte. It had no interest for him. Just another town. In the fading light of day there was the outline of stores, the sky-jutting sweep of roof-tops, holes of blackness indicating alley-mouths, the broad dark carpet of the two wide streets ... people walking, horses tethered, a buckboard disturbing the night with its wheel-creaking sound.

The town meant nothing to him because his mind's eye, as always, was fixed on something else, something he wanted, faint and indistinct in outline. Once that something had shape and form and color, depth, meaning. He doubted if it would ever take real shape again. Louise Yerby was gone. She was not in this town. She was in no town. Time had stopped for her. Eternity had claimed her.

Sundown shifted impatiently under Durant so he leaned forward and stroked the stallion's sweat-slicked shoulder. The big black became quiet again, assured that everything was all right by the big man's gentle touch.

"Okay, boy, let's look it over."

Sundown nickered and Durant gave rein. They went down the trail and into the town of Glory Creek. Now Durant pulled himself out of the past and faced the present. He saw a marker indicating that J. B. Holmer tended horses at the most reasonable prices in town. Durant put Sundown into an alley-way. At the end of it he found a barn with night yards back of it and a line of stalls in an adjacent building. The establishment looked well kept.

Coming off Sundown, he led the big black into the light. The smell of hay brought up Sundown's head, sent his nostrils flaring. Blake removed the saddle as a bow-legged attendant, shirtless, came out of the depths of the barn. He was a middle-aged man with a gaunt face, shallow chest, sloped shoulders. His lusterless gaze lifted to Blake's sun-baked face and then swung to take in the horse. His lips pursed and his eyes widened a little.

"Come aways, eh?"

"Some distance, yeah." Blake tilted his flop-brimmed hat to the back of his head.

The attendant reached out for Sundown's bridle but the big black minced away. The attendant dropped his hand to his side. "Got fresh hay and oats," he said.

"Plenty of oats. He's travelled hard."

The attendant nodded and his look became more serious. "Cost you two dollars, mister—in advance. Oats is hard to come by this time of the year. Had me a store of it, but what with the boom everybody's loose with money and figurin' to treat their horses best they can. Store's fast thinnin' down."

Blake fetched money from his pocket. "Give him a rubdown, good oats, and leave him plenty of room to move. Don't try to handle him much. He's a one-man horse."

Blake pulled his hide coat from his shoulders and slapped range dust from it. Then he removed his bandanna and crossed to a trough on the other side of the barn. He dipped the golden bandanna into the water, wrung it partly dry and replaced it on his neck. As he went on his way, looking for drink for himself and some food, he heard the attendant mutter:

"Hoss, you found yourself a good feed, you'll see. So you behave. Quit shiftin' now."

Blake liked the confident sound of the man's voice and worried no more about Sundown. Not that he ever did worry much ... somehow the blue-black stallion always fixed things to his own liking. Between man and horse there was an attachment that no pressure, no hardship, could destroy. They had been too many places together, had known too many different trails.

Blake headed back up the laneway towards the front street. It was night now and the glow from the oil lights cut across the alley's opening. Sounds came in from the street, the ordinary sounds of townspeople living out another evening of their monotonous lives. Blake pulled a pouch from his shirt pocket and stopped to build a cigarette.

His attention was suddenly attracted by the fleeting, furtive movement of somebody coming

into the laneway. The figure flattened against
the wall and the oval face of a young woman was
caught in the flow of street light. Blake saw dark
brown hair, small features. A pretty girl. But it
was a face full of worry. Suddenly she flattened
against the wall and her body tensed. Durant
heard her gasp.

He looked in the direction of her gaze. Three
figures loomed up, two close together, one hesi-
tantly trailing. The woman sidled along the alley
wall, ignorant of Durant's presence.

Blake studied the three men. Streetlight
gleamed from the bald head of one and high-
lighted his narrow forehead, small mouth and
pointed chin. His clothes were grubby and
untidy on his long, lean frame. The man beside
him was much the same. He held his left shoulder low, positioning his right hand just above
his gun butt. The third was a runt, with a round,
apprehensive face, sagged mouth and a look of
uncertainty.

They were walking towards the frightened
young woman when Blake lit his cigarette. The
girl turned as the flame attracted her attention.

"You all right, ma'am?" he asked.

The girl took several quick steps towards him.
"Please help me."

"Sure." He moved to the mouth of the alley, the cigarette smoking in his hand. The two men stopped in their tracks. The third stood back and sucked on his teeth noisily.

"You there, you keep out of this!" came from the middle man.

He threw a look at his companion and motioned with his right hand. His companion came two more steps into the alley then stopped as the sound of a ruckus came from the boardwalk behind him. He wheeled and was immediately knocked backwards by the weight of a man crashing into him. Both of them went down. Blake Durant eyed the first man, seeing the anger and annoyance rise in his face. His hand went to his gun butt. The runt against the wall let out a terrified howl as four big men came bustling against him. Caught in the brawling melee, he went down and crawled through legs. Blake made no move. The young woman came against him and her frightened face lifted towards him. Wide eyes studied him apprehensively. She was trembling.

Blake Durant said, "Stand still. Nobody will hurt you."

Another three men came charging off the boardwalk. Foul curses rose above the explosion of punches and grunts. The runt had found clear space on the other side of the alley and stood with his hands pressed against the wall, much the same as the young woman had. Blake gave him a casual look and concentrated on the other two. Caught in the swirl of bodies, both were cursing. Baldy, grasped by the shirt, was dragged forward. Two punches narrowly missed his ducking head. He lashed out angrily and got a smack in the mouth for his trouble. More men thundered along the boardwalk.

Blake, taking advantage of the fight, grasped the woman's hand and led her back into the gloomy depths of the alley. Fifteen yards away from the brawl he stopped and smoked, his face lined with concentration.

"Who are the three men?" he asked.

She shook her head and the clean scent of pine came from her. He saw that she was slender in the right places.

"I don't know," she whispered as if afraid somebody might overhear her. "They've been following me for days and days. Everywhere I go."

Blake nodded and stamped on his cigarette. The brawling mob had gone past the alley and were still slugging it out. Then the two tall, lean men came bursting through the melee of punches, lashing legs, rolling and falling bodies. The runt followed, but feet behind, shuffling with urgency.

Away from the trouble, the bald-headed man stopped. His eyes shone fiercely. He regarded Blake heavily for a moment, then snapped out a curse.

"You! Git!"

Blake shook his head slowly. The young woman noticed that his hands were slack in front of his waist. Yet she had the feeling that those hands knew where the holsters were. Blake's face was expressionless.

"Mister, you're out of your depth," he said.

A twist of worry worked across the bald-headed man's weathered wolfish face. His lean shoulders squared. His mouth moved and sullen sounds came from him. Then his right hand swept down. Blake Durant dropped his hand and the gun came swinging up. He put a shoulder partly in front of the young woman.

"Don't be a fool," he said tightly.

The lean man's hand stopped on the gun butt. His companion's hand had stopped short on his holstered Colt. The runt floundered to a halt, tripping into the back of the man on the right. A growl and an elbow push sent him reeling into the wall. Behind them the brawling crowd had gone along the boardwalk and their curses were dying in the deepening silence of the street.

The young woman worked herself a little more behind Blake and said urgently, "Ask them who they are. Find out what they want of me."

Blake nodded. He left her and walked towards the trio. As he drew closer, coming out of the deep shadows, the two tall men gasped and exchanged a hurried look.

Then, "Ragnall!"

Blake allowed a slight frown to pucker his brow. At the same time he heard the woman gasp. Then she came to his side and peered curiously at him, the fear leaving her face.

Blake asked, "Who the hell are you and what do you want with this woman?"

The tall man licked at his lips nervously. The runt stood wiping his face on his sleeve. Smears of dust blotted his pinched face. When Blake got no answer, he added, "Seems you've made a mistake. Back off and leave her be, now and later."

The runt was the only one to move. But a vicious look from the other two stopped him in his tracks. The runt's face twisted painfully and he shook his head desperately, spluttering out incoherent noise.

Blake stepped towards them. They backed off, shouldering each other out of the way. Blake crowded them to the main street. His gun stayed fixed on them as they turned and hurried off, grumbling. On the boardwalk, the two tall men hesitated but when Blake lifted his gun and the hammer clicked back, they continued to retreat, with the runt already ahead of them. Blake waited until they disappeared into the shadows beyond the saloon before he turned back. The young woman had followed close behind and now she swept her hair back and regarded him with more composure. The hint of a nervous smile began to break the rigidness of her mouth.

"I thought you'd never come," she said. She let out a deep sigh of relief and began to tidy her hair again. Then she worked on her clothes, tightening the silk blouse across her high, full breasts. She colored a little when she saw Blake's look go to her bust. But the guarded smile remained.

"I'm staying at the rooming house, Mr. Ragnall. We can go there. We must talk."

Blake looked back down the boardwalk. Ragnall? He couldn't pick the name from his memory. The trio of hardcase individuals had stopped just past the saloon and were bunched, watching him closely. But they kept their hands away from their guns. He drew in a ragged breath and asked:

"Where is the rooming house, ma'am?"

"Up here."

The young woman went a couple of paces past him before she stopped and turned back. Uncertainty worried her beautiful face.

"I'm Angela," she said. "Angela Grant."

Blake nodded at this information. He checked again on the rough-bred trio and saw them inching closer. Blake took the young woman's arm and steered her off.

"We'd best talk indoors. They've still got an itch in them."

Angela stiffened as his powerful grip took hold. But after the first slight drawing back she allowed Blake to escort her down the boardwalk. They passed a few townspeople who looked at each of them in turn. A big woman gave them an approving smile. At the rooming house, Blake let her step before him, and following, removed his hat. He ran leather toughened fingers through his thick yellow hair and took the foyer in. It was deserted except for a clerk busy at a desk ledger. Blake pointed to a seat by the window and followed her across, noticing that she had the normal woman's way of fussing with her person. The light came onto her face again and he was surprised to find her features slightly familiar. There was a proud tilt to her head. She had a small upturned nose, a soft, mobile

15

mouth. There was a gentle expression in her brown eyes.

"First thing we have to get straight, Miss Grant, is that I'm not Ragnall. Name's Blake Durant."

Her stare became troubled. The self-possession which he'd seen taking hold of her was immediately shattered.

"I don't understand," she said. "Back there—"

"They called me Ragnall, Miss Grant. I didn't figure it mattered at the time. Now how about telling me what it's all about? If they mean to pester you some more, we'll call in the law."

Angela clasped her hands on her lap. Her cool eyes, the color of drought grass, disconcerted him somewhat by reflecting a smile. She touched at her hair again, putting a soft ringlet back into place.

"You'll think me a fool," she said, and when the warmth in her eyes died, she added, "Or worse."

Blake sat down, still watching the street. The cut of the trio in the laneway had told him that they were no more than bullies on the prod. He dismissed them from his mind and looked more intently at her. She wasn't really pretty, he decided. But she had an appeal which was beginning to get its hooks into him. Perhaps it was sympathy, he told himself.

"Just tell it from the beginning. If I can help, I will. Don't worry about time. That's something I have plenty of."

"Thank you," she said and lowered her gaze to her hands. She sat very still and Blake had the impression she was collecting her thoughts. He waited.

TWO

"PA!"

In the street two lawmen had broken up the cowhands' brawl. Blake overheard a thick-voiced man issuing a warning to a bunch of battered, bleeding men. Within minutes, the trouble-makers shuffled off, divided into two groups, one moving west and the other east.

"I was so relieved when those men called you Mr. Ragnall, Mr. Durant. I thought all my waiting was over."

"Waiting, Miss Grant?"

Blake divided his attention between her and the street outside. The trio had evidently gone off when the lawmen arrived. It told him just a little more about them.

She pinched her lips a little and worked her hands about on her lap. Her voice, deep and husky, went on:

"I've been waiting for Zeb Ragnall. I'd arranged to meet him here in Glory Creek. I drove all the way from Cheyenne, through some of the most terrifying towns I've ever seen. It was in Barnaby that those three men first showed an interest in me, and they've turned up everywhere I've gone since then. Tonight was the first time, though, that they attempted to speak to me."

Blake frowned, considering what she said. Then, "If you came to meet Ragnall, how come you mistook me for him? Surely the light wasn't that bad."

Color rose in her cheeks. "I—I've never met him before."

Her eyes settled on his face, then her gaze dropped away. "Mail bride?" he asked.

Her brown eyes were troubled again. "I suppose you might call it that, Mr. Durant. You see, I answered an advertisement in the Cheyenne Post. Mr. Ragnall had inserted it, asking for communication with any young woman who might be interested in coming out this way. I wrote back, telling him I was interested and asking for more details. We communicated three times after that.

He told me he was a miner, that he'd struck it rich and could see no sense in having money unless there was somebody to share it with. Judging by his letters, he's well educated and sincere."

Blake nodded. He'd heard it all before. Although some lasting contacts had been made in that way, mutual happiness for the parties involved was not the usual result.

"This is hardly the kind of territory for a young woman to come to alone," he said.

"Mr. Ragnall sent me money for a new buckboard and expenses. He had pressing business which would not allow him to come to Cheyenne. My brother was ailing again so I decided to take my courage in both hands and—"

"Brother?"

She nodded, her face solemn. "My young brother. He is very sick. He needs hospitalization all the time. And that requires a lot of money. I mentioned all this to Mr. Ragnall in my second letter. He was very sympathetic and more than willing to help. He told me to get my brother settled as I liked and he'd fix the bills when they came in. I was so relieved. It was the first time anybody has done a kind thing for me or for my brother. I just had to take the chance."

Blake drew easily on his cigarette. "What's wrong with your brother, Miss Grant?"

"He has consumption. When Pa died, I didn't know what to do. I was engaged to be married but when Lee, my fiancé, found out about my brother, he went away. I never heard from Lee again."

Tears formed in her eyes. Durant stood up and pinched out his cigarette. As he tossed the butt out the window he made another check of the street. It was empty.

"So you came here and Ragnall hasn't showed up yet. When is he due?"

"He said he'd meet me here as soon as he could." Her eyes clouded with worry again but she managed a small smile. "I'll be all right, Mr. Durant. I've caused you enough trouble. However, I am worried about those three men. I don't know why they should want to bother me."

"I'll handle them," he said. "You fixed okay for money, Miss Grant?"

Angela lifted her head and smiled warmly. "Yes. But thank you. You've been very kind."

Blake shifted his gunbelt higher on his waist. "You have any more troubles, call in the law. By the sound of the sheriff outside a while back, he can handle those three jaspers in a blink. Better still, stay indoors and wait for Ragnall. If I hear he's in town, I'll find him and send him on."

"Thank you again." Angela held out her hand. Blake looked thoughtfully at her for a moment, then shook her hand. Her eyes stayed fixed on him.

"Everybody needs somebody," he said. "Don't let anybody shift you off from what you've decided to do."

He went on his way, leaving her staring curiously after him. The way he had stood up to the three troublemakers had impressed Angela Grant a great deal. Now she sat and listened to his firm footsteps on the boardwalk outside. She presumed he would go to the saloon and drink. He looked to be that kind of man, a man's man.

Who exactly was he? The question disturbed her. He had come out of the night and had calmly taken charge of things. She wondered if she had expressed her gratitude sufficiently. But then she realized that his abrupt manner had kept her from saying more. He had a hard way about him, but he wasn't cruel. She felt that he had had more than his share of suffering.

Angela sighed and settled back as the night grew quiet around her. She thought of Zeb Ragnall, wondering what he was like. His letters had told her little, but then she had never taken much notice of anybody's talk. It was what a person did that counted.

Perhaps Ragnall had changed his mind about meeting her here. As this thought struck Angela, she gasped and felt alone, miserably alone. Blake Durant had offered her money. Perhaps, she should have accepted. Then she stood up, smoothed down her frock again and chided herself for being a fool. She had come this far to meet Zeb Ragnall. All right; she would meet him and make the most of it. Her brother was really the one who counted. He had to be looked after. Later, perhaps, when he got a little better, he could come and join them. She crossed to the foyer clerk and picked up her key.

As she turned away, the clerk said, "Going to be a hot night, Miss Grant, but I wouldn't open my window if I were you. Lot of damn hellions gettin' drunk in town; could be some trouble later."

Angela thanked him and went up the stairway to her room.

"It's him all right," said bald-headed Mark Madie. "No doubt about it. I seen him ride in on that big black. Matthew mentioned that, didn't he—a big man, wide, ridin' a black?"

"Lots of black stallions in the territory," his brother Luke said.

In the background stood the runt, John Madie, peering nervously at them while he picked his nose.

Mark gave an angry snort. "I know damn well there's a lot of black horses. But he went straight up to that woman, that Miss Grant, didn't he? Got her away from us, damn him to hell and gone!"

"Pa said we shouldn't cuss, Mark," put in John Madie. "And you just cussed. Pa hears you, he'll skin you."

Mark turned on his young brother and scowled. "I said for you to shut down, damn you, John. I'm sick of hearin' you talk about pa. Pa this, pa that. Shut your miserable flap!"

John took a backward step and wiped his nose on his sleeve. "Just tellin' you, Mark," he whimpered. "If pa heard you, he'd go for all of us. You know how pa is."

"I know how pa is, and I know how you are, blast you! Git lost! Luke and me got things to discuss. Git now!"

John went another couple of backward steps. His face was pale and his skinny hands shook. The wind whipping down the street plastered his shirt to his sunken chest. He was inches shorter than either of his brothers and looked a pathetic creature with his clothes hanging limp on a body that was more bone than flesh. He eyed them miserably, swallowed a few times and finally found words.

"I just figured—"

"You ain't got nothin' to figure with. Get washed. You stink to hell."

Mark took a threatening step towards John and the runt turned quickly and picked his way along the boardwalk. At the saloon doors, he stopped and looked fearfully back. His brothers were staring sourly at him. He entered the saloon and immediately had to dodge out of the way of two big cowhands heading for the batwings. Muttering, glancing in all directions and sniffing loudly, he reached the saloon counter. He pulled out some change, counted it twice, then looked up in alarm as the big apron stopped before him.

"If you ain't drinkin', mister, step away and let those who are get in to me."

John looked at his money again and shakingly pushed it forward. The barkeep dug a finger through the coins, picked up most of them, then filled a glass with rye. He gave John a disgusted sniff and went on to serve other customers. John picked up his drink, looked nervously about him, and sipped at the whisky. Then he lowered the glass and looked at himself in the bar mirror. His wrinkled face looked like a thrown-away boot. He didn't care. He'd never cared about himself, only about pa. Pa was coming and when pa heard about Matthew being killed, Luke knew all hell would break loose. His nose was running again, as it mostly was, so he wiped it dry with his sleeve. A big man shouldered past him and Luke was propped into the swill of noisy drinkers. He looked about for more room for himself and hoped Mark and Luke would hurry. Then he saw the big man who'd helped the Grant woman. He was standing alone at the other end of the counter, emptying a glass down his throat. John turned and broke into a run. He bumped into men on his staggering, dodging way to the swing doors, and curses rained after him.

On the boardwalk, he looked about anxiously for his brothers. Dirty sweat ran down his face and he sleeved it off. His tattered shirt flapped against his skinny frame as he went down the boardwalk in search of his brothers, limping because he had lost a heel on the boards coming out of the saloon. He looked down at his scuffed boots and moaned.

Pa would be mad. Pa was always mad when he wore something out. John gulped, wiped away more sweat, then dug his nails into the palms of his skinny hands and limped on, muttering about his bad luck.

Mark and Luke Madie had gone fifty yards down the street, and now they nervously watched a group of close-bunched cowhands who were in turn watching two lawmen making their rounds of the street. The angry murmurs from the group warned Mark and Luke that these hard-cases meant trouble for somebody. They wanted no part of it.

A freighter clattered along, lifting dust from the wide street. A woman giggled as she went past, pressed close to a tall townsman who looked anxiously about him as if afraid he might be followed. When they turned into an alleyway, Mark muttered:

"No mistakin' what they're up to, eh?"

Luke nodded. His eyes had devoured the young woman's lushly curved body and it brought on the memory of the one woman he'd slept with. Desire churned inside him. He cursed. One damn woman in his whole life, and no likelihood of finding another, not the way pa kept badgering them, watching them, damning them to hell if they as much as looked at a woman's ankle.

"When we fix Ragnall, I'm gonna skit off," Luke said. I'm goin' to a town where nobody knows me, and don't know pa, and where pa can't find me. Gonna get me a woman and a good drink and maybe I'll gamble some. Damn it, I'm twenty-nine and I never knowed hardly any fun."

Luke scrubbed a hand across his grubby neck and looked bleakly about, keeping tab on the cowhands. He heard the creak of leather behind him but ignored the sound. Then something hit him in the middle of the back and sent him sprawling. He let out a howl of protest as he slammed into the wall and nearly broke both wrists stopping his momentum. He heard a yell from Mark, then Mark crashed against him. Pushing his brother away, Luke scrambled to his feet. His face was flushed with anger that died almost at birth. His mouth gaped.

"Idlin', like you always done, both of you. Never a day in your lives have you known the sweat of toil which cleanses the body, the mind and the soul!"

Mark was also speechless at the sight of the man astride the pure white stallion, a huge and powerful man, garbed in severe black.

"Pa!"

"Minds contaminated with evil! Eyes which see nothing but the vices of the world! Mouths dirty with desire! Disciples of the devil!"

The big man's voice bellowed across the boardwalk and Luke and Mark stood huddled together, hands at their sides, looking miserably up at him. Isaac Madie dismissed them with another seething look and turned his attention to the town about him. His big jowls bulged with disapproval. His eyes sank back in his head and his bushy brows came down. Then a rumble of noise came from his deep chest.

"Sinners' paradise! Sodom and Gomorrah!" was his final opinion as he heaved his weight out of the saddle. Luke came forward to take the reins of the horse and hitch it to the rail. Mark stood back, licking nervously at his lips.

"Pa! Pa!"

John Madie came running down the board-walk, his face afire with excitement. Isaac Madie watched him come, his fat lips curled back in a sneer, his sunken eyes glaring at the slight figure of his third son. He noticed that John's clothes were a little more tattered, his shirt torn at one shoulder, and something was wrong with one of his boots. John skidded to a halt, grinning sheep-ishly. Isaac Madie's nostrils quivered and he reached out and pulled John to him. He put his nose close to his son's mouth and fierce anger rose in his throat.

"Drink!" he roared. "Hell's brew!"

John let out a whimper as the big man's strong hands almost crushed his arm. Then he found himself lifted from the boardwalk. Isaac Madie stormed down the street until he came to a trough. He plunged John's head into it, and kept ducking him until finally he cast the spluttering, half-drowned youth to the dusty street.

"One week away from my guidance and Satan gets his hooks into you!" Isaac wheeled about, his big boots grating on the warped boards. He pulled Mark to him and heaved him against the wall of the store. He went to grab for him again but Mark dodged away and stood beside Luke, trying to push in behind him.

Mark said, "Ease off, Pa, you got it all wrong. We had to keep going after what we learned."

"'Bout Matthew," Luke put in nervously.

"Better for me to have cast my seed on the barren ground than to be cursed with the likes of you," growled the big man. He moved in closer and John cringed. Isaac cuffed him upright and when John whimpered Isaac blew out a hot breath. "I did my best, as the good Lord knows, and now I stand before Him to do my penance for failure. As you will, too! Pray for salvation, ye sinners! Pray to the good Lord and beg His forgiveness! Bow your heads and—!"

"Matthew's dead," Luke said abruptly.

Isaac stood there, battered Bible pressed against his broad chest. His whole body stiffened and his head came down, the muscles on his neck puffing out. His look went to Luke and settled there, a fire flaming in his eyes.

"What did you say, boy?"

"Matthew, he's gone, Pa. Was killed back in Cheyenne."

"And we been followin' a woman to get a bead on his killer, Pa," said Mark. "All the way to here. Sent you word."

John sniffed and wiped water from his face and hair. He sleeved his nose and coughed. When his father's look burned at him, he nodded urgently and whimpered, "All the way, Pa, three of us, lookin' for him."

"Quiet, boy," growled Isaac Madie. He thumped the Bible into his left palm and the sound made John jump. Isaac then studied his two older sons and finally he nodded at Luke. "You talk now, and nothin' fancy and no lies. If my boy's dead, then I want to know the absolute truth of it."

Mark mopped at his bald head as Luke spoke. "We was ridin' into Cheyenne when Matthew caught up with us, Pa. He had two bullets in him and was dyin'. We did the best we could for him, but he was goin' fast. We buried him on that slope we prayed on alongside you, Pa, before ridin' into Cheyenne."

Isaac's face turned gray and his eyes went cold. A nerve jumped at his temple. When he said nothing, Luke went on quickly:

"Afore he died, Pa, he—"

"He was christened Matthew and blessed with the name of Madie. Call my son right, boy!"

"Sure, Pa, sure, I forgot," Luke apologized. "Matthew, afore he died, he told us somethin'. He was caught up in a robbery with a man named Ragnall. They ... they robbed the Wells Fargo office in Cheyenne, Pa!"

Isaac stepped forward and caught his son by the throat. "What's that, boy? You brand your brother a thief? You've become a Cain to your brother?"

Luke choked and tried to grunt out a reply, but his father's fingers were closed tight on his windpipe.

"Speak, boy! You claimin' my boy was an agent of the devil?" Isaac shook Luke whose eyes seemed ready to pop from his head.

Mark said quickly, "Luke is right, Pa. Hell, Matthew told us himself. He damn well said it as plain as—"

Isaac released Luke and hit Mark with a back-hand. When Mark gaped back at him, he howled, "No cussin', I told you! I told you not to use any words that ain't written in the Good Book. I got to beat your fool head in to make you understand? One boy an agent of the devil and you cussin' and him snivellin' and Luke lyin'." Isaac rolled his eyes heavenward. "Why, Lord, why?"

After a moment's spluttering to regain his breath, Luke grated out, "I ain't lyin', Pa. It's God's honest truth."

Isaac shuddered as if somebody was raking his body with hellfire. He continued to stare into the dark sky above, moving his lips soundlessly. Then he raised the Bible to his lips and kissed it. Finally he turned back to them, his face more composed but his stare just as fierce.

"I'll have it all now, Luke, but no interruptions from cussers or snivellers. None, you hear?"

John nodded so hard he hurt his neck. Mark merely gave an affirmative grunt and rubbed his jaw where his father's backhand had struck him.

Luke cleared his throat. "Like I said, Pa, Matthew and Ragnall robbed the Wells Fargo office and Matthew was to meet up with Ragnall once they gave the posse the slip. He did that and got two bullets for his trouble. But Matthew said, afore he died, that Ragnall was easy to pick—a big man riding a black and headin' west. So we sent word on to you and came after him. Sure enough we picked up his trail and we darned near cornered him in Barnaby in a hotel."

"Near?" Isaac barked.

Luke coughed again. "Seen him going into the hotel and followed him to his room. When

33

we busted in he cleared out through the window and all we seen was the back of him."

"Fools!" Isaac thundered.

"We made him run, Pa. He went so fast he left his saddle pouches behind, and in one of them we found these here letters, addressed to him, Zeb Ragnall. So we was on the right trail, eh, Pa?"

Isaac plucked the three letters from Luke's hand and shoved him away roughly. "Boy, you never been right on one thing in your whole accursed life." He opened the envelopes and moved to read the letters under the oil pot street light. His three sons stood watching him, hardly daring to breathe in their terror of him. After a few minutes, Isaac came back to them and growled out:

"This woman, this Miss Angela Grant. What of her?"

"She's in town here, Pa," Luke said, brightening. "We missed Ragnall in Barnaby, but we picked up his trail right enough just outside the town. And, like it says in them there letters, Miss Grant was to come here by buckboard and meet him. Well, we high-tailed it here and seen her drive in, buckboard and all, and later a jasper riding a big black came in, only we wasn't sure, as Mark said, if it was Ragnall. But when we challenged this Grant woman, this feller came packin' a gun and forced us off. We been waitin' for him to show again, only you showed up first, Pa. What do you want us to do now?"

"That feller's in the saloon," John put in quietly.

Isaac swung fiercely to him. "What's that, boy?"

John gulped. The wind flapped his shirt and trough water sprayed over Mark's boots. John pointed over his shoulder. "In the saloon, Pa. I just seen him. I came out to tell Mark and Luke."

Isaac breathed a long sigh, then he stuffed the letters in his pocket, straightened his black string tie and patted trail dust from his trousers and black silk coat. After that he opened the Bible and thumbed through the pages before he read aloud:

"Prepare ye the way of the Lord."

He lifted his head and his three sons stood in silent attention, listening to his muttering. When he finished, Isaac turned and strode down the boardwalk with his sons trailing. At the batwing doors, he glanced back at them, gave a contemptuous snort at the bedraggled John and said:

"What we do now will be the work of the Lord. Sinner for sinner and both to dust. Point him out."

Luke and Mark exchanged a worried look but Isaac grabbed them both and pitched them into the saloon. When John went to hurry past, the big man planted himself in the doorway. John bumped into him and was knocked aside. Ignoring his son's cry of pain, Isaac went inside.

THREE

"FOOLS!"

The saloon was packed as Luke and Mark Madie were pitched headlong into the throng. The earlier brawl had whetted the customers' appetites for excitement and two men coming headlong and skidding on their chests suited them just fine. Then the mountainous figure of Isaac Madie loomed inside the doorway and silence fell. Isaac let his scathing look sweep the crowd, contempt in his face for each and every one of them. Luke and Mark struggled to their feet and Isaac said, "Where is he?"

The two tall sons wiped the sawdust off their clothes and looked about them. Then John came alongside Isaac and pointed towards the end of the bar counter where Blake Durant stood, a glass in one hand, a cigarette in the other. Cowhands flanked him but his striking figure stood out against the nondescript crowd. Isaac's brow rutted and his teeth bared.

He grabbed John by the scruff of the neck and lifted him off the floor. "Where, boy?"

"There, Pa, the big man. It's him."

Isaac let out a blast of words and hurled him away. Then he grabbed Luke and Mark and pushed them against the counter.

"Him?" he asked, pointing a massive finger at Blake. "That's your Zeb Ragnall?"

"Yeah, Pa, it's him all right," Luke said. "Him who killed Matthew."

Isaac let out a growl and slammed their heads together. John had regained his balance, and now he stood behind his father.

"Take care, Pa, he's right handy with a gun," John advised. "And tricky, you can bet."

Isaac sideswiped him away and regarded Blake Durant grimly. "Seems there's been some mistake made against you, Durant, by these snivellin' scum I got landed with. If you'll bide your time, I'll fix it proper in the true justice of the Lord."

Isaac turned and pulled Luke and Mark together again. He gave John a nudge in the ribs and made him rise from the floor. They had a great deal of room now, with the crowd backed off, most of them watching in amusement. Isaac shook Luke and Mark until their hats fell off and their hair fell loose about their faces. When he stopped, he held them towards Blake Durant and said:

"This here's Mr. Blake Durant, you fools. Durant, who happened by my place when you was skulkin' in the dirty shadows of a sin town leavin' me to sweat till I near dropped keeping things together for you. Now look good and never forget this man who is as blessed with goodness as you scum are cursed with badness."

Isaac grabbed John and hurled him at the other two and when they fell against the counter, he switched his Bible to his left hand and pushed the hand towards Durant.

Blake Durant accepted the handshake and said, "Howdy, Madie."

"Durant, I'm bedeviled by fools of sons. They figured you for a man named Ragnall, the murderer of my other son, Matthew, in Cheyenne."

Blake looked at the thoroughly depressed Luke and Mark. "I figured there was some mistake."

"Mistakes are their habit, Durant. Mistakes are what they fatten on, one stupidity after another.

Their minds are filled with the foulness of what they see about them, and they can't climb above it." Isaac Madie turned and swept an empty rye glass off the counter. It smashed at John Madie's feet, causing him to shrink again, so frightened that saliva glistened at the corners of his gaping mouth. The skin of his face was stretched taut, as if there was barely enough of it to cover the bones.

Isaac pulled Luke to him and pointed at the rye-stained bar counter. "Buy, boy, sarsaparilla, all round! Then beg forgiveness from your Maker for not making anything of the chances He gave you."

Isaac pushed his three sons together and turned back to Blake. "It's not the failures I fret about, Durant. Far be it for me to fret on any account. Manna comes or it doesn't. A man must make his way with what the good Lord decrees is just for him. He must sweat and toil for the betterment of those placed under his care. He must stand solid to see that the fresh, clean air of the world is not stenched by the aroma of sin. He must do what he must."

Blake sipped his drink. Isaac Madie cast a glance at the glass and licked his lips. Then he settled back against the counter and eyed the onlookers defiantly. Under his glare the hard-bitten men shuffled their feet a bit and then returned to their own interests.

"And so, out of evil there is sometimes good, Durant," the old gray-haired man went on. He put his Bible on the counter and patted it. "In there is truth and guidance for those who want to pay heed. I am obligated to you, mister, and I have never forgotten that obligation. So tell me what you have been doing, a man like you, who will sweat beside an old man in need, who will share his food, share his thoughts and who will maybe one day kneel beside him at the altar of Him who counts."

Luke was still clearing his throat and Mark was rubbing his jaw where the brick-like side of Isaac's palm had struck him. John crouched beyond them, adoring eyes on his father, the earlier abuse forgotten.

Isaac broke the silence when he asked again, "What have you been doing with yourself, Durant?"

"Nothing much," Blake said. "Just driftin'."

Isaac's lips curled a little and his look hardened, but there was no strict censure in his gaze. "About my boys and the trouble they caused you ... That's what I want to know about, Durant. I reared fools and now I stand for them because they're too stupid to stand for themselves."

Blake saw Mark and Luke Madie scowl. John, however, did nothing more than hang on his father's words, all the time wiping his nose with his sleeve.

"They didn't cause me too much trouble," Blake said. "Forget it, Madie."

"Forget? Forget when the brand of hell is upon them? I've cast sinners out of my house, Durant, and would do the same to kin proved bad. Tell me the truth and they'll pay. They'll do their penance, I swear."

"No matter now," Blake said. "Just keep them away from Miss Grant."

"I want to know, mister!" Isaac Madie slammed his fist down on his Bible. His eyes were wild again. Blake shrugged.

"Okay, if it's what you want. I rode into town, stabled my horse, came into the saloon laneway and saw your boys crowding a young woman. I naturally took her part."

"Crowdin'? How far did they go?"

"Only as far as I let them. No harm done."

Isaac Madie nodded acceptance of this. "Couldn't shine your boots proper, Durant, what I seen of you a half year ago. This Ragnall now, how come you got mistook for him?"

"I don't know, Madie. Look, let's just forget it. All I want to do is get the saddle cramp out of me, have some good grub and stretch out. So take your boys home."

Isaac Madie shook his head stubbornly. "Ain't a one of us goin' home till we find the murderin' scum who killed my other boy. Set myself to have four sons, and I got 'em. Named 'em after the finest men ever to set foot on this earth, barrin' the One. Matthew, Mark, Luke and John. You've heard of 'em, Durant ... a man like you, trimmed down for hard work, keen-minded for good living, you'd have heard."

Blake shrugged.

"I'll see the woman," Isaac announced. "And then I'll find the murdering scum my boys followed to this town. For the trouble they caused you, Blake Durant, you've got my most sincere apology. It will not happen again, this I swear."

Isaac turned, grabbed Mark and Luke and heaved them away. John stepped back quickly. "Git!" Isaac shouted. "Git and find a place to kneel and turn your eyes to heaven and speak the words of the Good Book till your throats are dry."

He laid the Bible onto Luke's and Mark's backs and sent them staggering away, hands held protectively above their heads. A roar of laughter came from a group of cowhands, but this changed to a howl of anger and pain as Mark,

falling, buried an elbow into a big man's groin.
The cowhand hurled his glass aside and plucked
Mark from the floor. He brought back his hand,
meaning to punch the stuffing out of Mark,
when Isaac seized John and hurled him at the
pair of them. Mark and his assailant went down,
the cowhand cursing. Isaac moved forward,
shouldering another two men aside. He grabbed
the cowhand and hurled him across the counter
with one effortless heave. Then he grabbed Mark
and pitched him towards the swing doors, calling
out:

"Begone, Satan, to the fires that await you!"

Luke came up fast as a second cowhand lunged
at his father, but before Luke could throw a blow
a punch split his mouth open. He was reeling
when Isaac caught him by the forearm and pro-
pelled him after Mark. Luke's feet left the boards
and he collected a staggering, whimpering John
on the way and carried him across the saloon.
Isaac then brought his huge left fist down on
the second cowhand's shoulder and drove him
to his knees. He kneed him in the face and
pronounced:

"He who lives by the sword shall perish by the
sword!"

He was turning away when the barkeep
shouted, "Hey, wait on there! This here cowboy

just broke three bottles of my best whisky, mister.
Somebody's got to pay."

"Your reward will be in the hereafter, mister,
since it is a fitting sacrifice for your sins."

Isaac picked John up from the floor, stead-
ied him, then drove a kick into his pants. John
yelped and went into the air but was soon on his
feet and running. When Isaac Madie breasted
wide the swing doors, he saw his three sons
scrambling to their feet. He eyed them wrath-
fully and without a word pounded off down the
boardwalk to the rooming house in search of
Miss Angela Grant.

Blake Durant grinned down at his glass. About
him a group of cowhands were cursing bitterly,
some wanting to go out and settle with the Bible-
toting old hardcase. The barkeep had helped the
unconscious cowboy to his feet and was trying to
shake him back into consciousness. Blood ran
down the big man's right cheek.

Blake drank and let the noise settle down.
He thought of the time he had spent with Isaac
Madie, on his place in the Sonora Valley, which
the old fox claimed as his own in defiance of
the law, the townspeople, neighboring ranch-
ers, and anybody who put foot on his soil. Blake
had come to like the old buzzard, despite his

over-zealous attention to the Bible's dictates. Underneath it all though, Isaac Madie was a conniving miser.

A tin star wearer entered the saloon and began talking to the barkeep. When Blake was pointed out to him, the lawman strode over. He eyed Blake speculatively for a moment before he leaned an elbow on the counter and flicked a coin towards the barkeep.

"Seems trouble finds you, mister," he said.

Blake shrugged. The lawman removed his hat to mop at his brow, then he took his drink and swilled it about in the glass. He was short, solid, and good looking. His dark hair was thinning in front and beginning to gray at the temples.

The lawman said, "There was trouble with the woman in the laneway, then that Bible-toter sought you out here. Mind if I ask you a few questions?"

"Ain't much to know," Blake said.

"I think that may be wrong. I saw you ride in. Come aways, eh?"

"Up through the Platte River country, across to Meredith, then south to here."

"Just lookin'?"

"Taking my fill of the country, yeah."

"Lookin' for work?"

Blake shrugged. "Yes and no."

The sheriff frowned and tugged at his chin before he sipped at his drink. He wasn't nearly as tall as Blake, but his eyes had a definite way of looking at a man. Blake held his gaze, the beginning of a smile touching at his mouth.

"Name's Blake Durant," he told the sheriff and extended his hand.

The lawman took it. "Sheriff Lasting, and I don't much go on cracks about the name. I was called Curly but that was before the mop began to thin out. Now we've got that settled, what's with the big man and his Bible?"

Blake took a sip of his drink before he said, "His name is Isaac Madie. I worked at his place about six months ago. His boys followed a man on a black stallion to this town and figured he was connected with a woman named Angela Grant. I don't know apart from that what it's all about, Lasting, except they took me for the other man."

Lasting had stiffened and frowned, as if the information meant plenty to him. "Mistake on their part, eh?"

"Yeah, a mistake."

Lasting screwed up his mouth and eyed the big Colt that nestled in Blake's right side holster. "Witness in the lane yonder said he seen you clear leather faster'n a rattler could strike."

47

"There are slow rattlers," Blake said.

Lasting grinned briefly. "Somebody else said you took that purty little woman to the rooming house, talked a time with her and then came down here. Then Madie showed with his boys and started to tear this place apart."

Blake chuckled. "He kicked his boys around for making a mistake about me, Sheriff. Maybe he tossed a cowboy across the bar, and maybe he asked for it. Don't do for anybody to buy into Isaac Madie's troubles, no matter which side they get on. He kinda explodes and doesn't care much who gets hurt, as long as what happens is his idea of the way of the Lord."

"Way of the ...?" Lasting scratched his head.

"Him and his Bible, they're quite a combination, Sheriff. But he doesn't do much more harm than bang a couple of heads when he gets going, unless maybe somebody crowds his kin. Then I guess he's just about like the rest of us."

Lasting shook his head. "What I heard, Durant, is a little different to that."

"Anybody get shot?" Blake asked. "Did you hear a shot?"

Lasting was forced to shake his head again.

"So no real harm was done, right?"

Blake finished his drink and stepped back from the counter. As far as he was concerned it was time for grub. Then he meant to look in on Sundown again and see that he was settled comfortably for the night before finding quarters for himself. So far Glory Creek had had its moments, more than enough to do him for the evening. He was turning away when Lasting dropped a restraining hand on his muscled forearm.

Blake looked calmly at the lawman.

"One thing you best know, Durant. Matthew Madie was killed a week ago—after he robbed the Wells Fargo office in Cheyenne."

Blake stiffened. "After, you said?"

"Yeah, after. Got clean away, him and his partner, who has since been identified as Ringo Nyall. Now ain't this all taking a real cute turn, Durant?"

Blake gave no answer.

Lasting grinned thinly. "Quite a rundown of facts, eh? Ringo Nyall and one of the Madie boys rob the Wells Fargo office in Cheyenne and clear off with forty thousand in gold bullion. Then Matthew Madie gets his comeuppance on his way home. Next thing I know, you turn up and get tangled in a young woman's affairs because you were mistaken for a man named Ragnall who the Madie boys are chasin' for killing their brother." Lasting sipped his drink and swilled the whisky around in his mouth. "You, Ragnall and Ringo Nyall ... that's some tie-up, ain't it?"

Blake shrugged. "Don't rope up the wrong bundle, Sheriff."

"Don't mean to. But what do you think of the next little point, Durant? You come in from the Platte River country which has Cheyenne beyond it. Then the Madie boys mistake you for the man who killed their brother. Now, I ain't found anybody who's seen or heard of a man called Zeb Ragnall supposedly riding a big black stallion ... same as the kind you're riding."

Blake drew in a ragged breath. "Don't trip on a root, Sheriff."

Lasting shook his head. "I'm tryin' not to, Durant. I'm a man who goes slow after his facts, but when I get 'em I act real quick. You understand?"

"Clearly, Sheriff." Blake thought for a moment. "You know, the way I see it, Zeb Ragnall could be this Ringo Nyall."

Lasting's mouth gaped and a hint of confusion showed in his green eyes. "Ragnall is Nyall?"

"Ragnall contacted Miss Grant and offered to marry her. How he meant to do that and when is his business and hers, I guess. But the Madie boys, following a man riding a black, called Zeb Ragnall, mistook me for him. Mistook is the key word there, Sheriff, so remember it. Later Isaac Madie arrived and cleared me before his sons. Which leaves you with only one thing to do."

"Tell it, Durant."

"You have to go off and locate Zeb Ragnall. Ragnall has been corresponding with Angela Grant and has made an appointment to meet her here in town. He told her in his letters that he is a miner who struck it rich. But maybe he did his mining in Cheyenne's main street and came up with a strike of gold bullion."

Lasting grunted thoughtfully. "Nyall."

"You got a description of him?" Blake asked.

Lasting nodded. "Word was sent to me along with the report of the robbery and the finding of Matthew Madie's grave outside Cheyenne. My information is that Nyall looks a lot like you ..."

Blake smiled. "There you are. The Madie bunch are hunting a man called Zeb Ragnall. Angela Grant is waiting here for Ragnall. I don't think anybody has to tell you what your next move should be."

Lasting straightened and adjusted his gun holster on his trim waist. "No, Durant, nobody has to tell me. I'll go and see the Grant woman. You come along."

Blake finished his drink and without argument led the way out of the saloon. On the boardwalk,

Lasting nudged Blake in the direction of the rooming house. As they walked along side by side the lawman kept watching Durant carefully, his hand resting on his gun butt. Blake noticed this but wasn't in the least worried.

In the rooming house foyer, Blake crossed to the desk and confronted the thin clerk. "Miss Grant in?"

The clerk checked Blake over and then gave his attention to Lasting. "Some trouble, Sheriff?"

"We want to see the Grant woman, Ben. What's the number of her room?"

"Was seventeen, Sheriff."

"Was?"

"She left a short time ago. Big man came in, asked for her, went up to her room. Short time later they came down with her bag. She paid her bill and they went out back. I saw this stranger fixing her buckboard, then she got in and they rode off, headin' north."

Lasting swore. "Towards the badlands, Ben? You sure of that?"

"Positive."

"Stranger sat with her, let her do the driving?"

Ben shook his head. "He trailed on his horse."

"Black stallion?" Lasting growled.

Ben showed surprise. "Why, yeah, big frisky fellow, long stride."

Lasting grunted his thanks and turned as Blake said, "Ragnall, alias Ringo Nyall."

Lasting's lips tightened. "Seems like."

"The girl came from Cheyenne and so did Nyall," Blake said. "Forty thousand dollars' worth of gold bullion is being toted through your territory, Lasting. How would you carry gold that heavy?"

Lasting scowled. "Buckboard."

Blake turned into the yard at the end of the foyer and looked north. Joining him, Lasting said, "Sure seems to fit, don't it? Nyall needed somebody to get a buckboard out here to him. So he fixed it for his woman to come and bring it. Meantime he's likely hidden the bullion someplace. Now they'll get it, stash it in the buckboard and kick their dust in our eyes." He swore savagely and punched the overhang post. "Damn it, the woman's in on it all the way through."

Blake shook his head. "I don't think so. I talked to her. She has family problems, needs money. As far as she knows, Zeb Ragnall is a miner who struck it rich. I doubt if she's ever heard of Ringo Nyall."

Lasting looked unconvinced. "Think what you like, Durant. Do what you like, too, because I reckon you're cleared."

53

"You'll need a posse," Blake said. "While you're getting it, I'll saddle up my horse and head out. My trail and theirs shouldn't be too hard to follow."

Lasting's scowl darkened. "How come it's your business, Durant? By hell, why should you buy in? Figure there's bounty at the end of it?"

"I'm worried about the girl. If this Ringo Nyall is only half the hellion you seem to think he is—"

"Hellion and worse, Durant! Ringo Nyall's about the scummiest damn jasper who ever threw a leg over a horse. Got a price on his head—robbery and murder."

"Then Miss Grant is in trouble, isn't she, Lasting? And time's short. I'll see you ... if you ever catch up."

Blake stepped into the yard and Lasting snapped, "Now hold on. I don't know as how I like you buttin' in. You want to come along, you can offer yourself for posse work."

Blake kept walking. At the yard gate he looked back. "If you run into Isaac Madie, best tell him what you've found out. Madie and his boys could come in right handy if you corner Nyall."

Blake used the back street to dodge the Madies, suspecting that another meeting with them would be of no advantage to him whatever. He reached the stable a few minutes later and saddled up Sundown. As he mounted the big black he heard shouting in the street. Then men were running towards the stable.

Blake hit Sundown into a run and the night swallowed him up as he left Glory Creek behind.

FOUR

CROWDED TRAIL

"What you reckon's goin' on, Pa?" Mark Madie asked the big man.

Isaac gave him no reply as he watched the men gathering outside the jailhouse. Luke was reclining against a store wall, pulling on his bottom lip and cursing his father under his breath for putting a welt over his right eye and bruising his left cheekbone. He swore he would cut out on his own just as soon as an opportunity presented itself.

"Find your brother and get your horses," Isaac said finally. "Be quick about it."

But even as the two brothers began to move away, John came running across the street from the end of town. He tripped over something in the dust, fell headlong, scrambled to his feet and raced full pelt towards his father and brothers.

Pulling up breathless, he gasped, "Pa, that Durant just rode out."

"I'm his keeper?" Isaac growled, twisting away to escape the odor coming from his youngest son's grubby body.

John frowned, unable to comprehend his father's meaning. Then, giving it up, he went on, "Seen him go with the sheriff into the rooming house, Pa. They talked to the clerk. I got real close and heard everything they said."

Isaac sighed mightily, glanced again at the men gathering outside the jailhouse, and snapped, "What did your sneak ears hear, boy?"

"The clerk, he said Miss Grant went off with a man riding a black horse, and she drove a buckboard. Mr. Durant, he said this was proof that Ragnall was Ringo Nyall."

"Nyall?" Isaac grabbed his son and pulled him close. John's shoulder stopped short of the big man's chest and he was forced to strain his neck to look up. "You tellin' me, boy, that there's talk of that scum Nyall bein' in these parts?"

John nodded, his head hitting his father's shirt buttons, and his running nose leaving a smear on the big man's shirt.

"Gone off with Miss Grant, Pa. Mr. Durant and the sheriff said was him who killed Matthew, robbed all that gold, and come here to marry Miss Grant. I come back as fast as I could, Pa, after I sorted it all out proper so I wouldn't make no mistake. I come fast, Pa, but I took my time all the same, not wantin' to tell you wrong."

Isaac pushed him away and growled at Luke and Mark, "Ain't you got them horses yet?"

The two brothers hurried off. John, eyes gleaming with satisfaction, stood on the board-walk's edge looking at his father expectantly. When Isaac ignored him, he said, "I did good, didn't I, Pa?"

Isaac's frowning face turned to John, who wiped his running nose on his sleeve and grinned stupidly. A grunt came from Isaac Madie as he kicked the feet from under his son. He went off as a startled cry came from the falling John. Walking down the street, Isaac looked towards the sky, closed his eyes and grumbled into the night, "If it be possible, let this cup pass from me. And let not my will, but Thine be done."

Blake Durant kept Sundown running. The big black, responding strongly, soon put miles behind Lasting's posse and Isaac Madie. If there was anybody he did not want cluttering up the range at the moment it was the big Bible basher, Madie and his three meddling sons.

Slowing Sundown, Durant topped a rise and stared across the wide, moon-raked prairie. For as far as he could see there was emptiness. And through the emptiness ran buckboard tracks, with the hoofmarks of a horse beside. Blake Durant gave Sundown a short breather, then set him into a steady canter until he saw the silver run of the river before him. Having come by this route to Glory Creek, Durant knew there was a bridge which crossed the deep river into the Badlands. It was dead country laid waste by seasonal droughts, and occupied by only itinerants and laze-abouts, men whose ambitions had been razed by failure.

Ten minutes later he reached the river, winding away to the south, a broad silver carpet whose surface was deceptively smooth. Below that surface he knew that hundreds of years of turmoil lay, snags shifting with the fast-running current, eddying pools through which even Sundown could not make progress. It was the kind of river a man would try to cross only in an extreme emergency.

But the bridge was there, made of strong planks, supported by huge pilings driven deep into the river bottom.

He rubbed Sundown's sweat-flecked shoulder and reined him in the direction of the bridge, hardly a quarter-mile away. Sundown, pleased to be held down to a walk, strode out freely as Blake followed the buckboard and single horse tracks which led straight for the bridge. He didn't know how much time he had made up on Ringo Nyall and Angela Grant, but he was confident that Sundown would catch up with them before morning.

Durant was within two hundred yards of the bridge when an explosion disturbed the peace of the night. Drawing rein, Blake saw the red flash, then timber was flying, huge chunks of seasoned lumber turning over and over in the clear moonlit air. Sundown shifted under him but Blake quietened him, swearing under his breath. It was not until the timber, rocks and mud had stopped falling that he saw the hunched-over figure of a man running along the opposite bank. Blake drew his gun, but even as he moved Sundown forward he knew a shot would be a waste of time. The figure disappeared from sight, then Blake heard the grind of buckboard wheels on hard ground. Moments later he saw the buckboard leave the cover of a clump of cottonwoods, a horse racing at its side.

Blake reached the river bank and drew rein. The bridge had lost its middle and both ends were no more than a twisted mess of splintered timber and shattered supports. A length of two-inch-thick cable wire was twisted around one ground bearer.

Blake muttered an oath as he studied the river. The water was running faster than it had when he came through the day before. He looked to the other bank; the buckboard and the rider were out of sight. Blade edged Sundown along the muddy bank. The only safe crossing was about fifteen miles further north. He headed Sundown that way. Nyall had gained a break on him, but with the girl and the buckboard to worry about on the desert, Blake was not too concerned about making up that lost time. When he finally caught up with Ringo Nyall, he'd have one more reason for taking the sass out of him.

Angela Grant slowed the buckboard up the rise, then suddenly drew the horses to a halt. In the wake of the buckboard, the big, haggard-faced rider swung wide and wheeled back. For a moment his eyes were filled with viciousness, but when Angela turned to look at him, his expression softened.

"What is it?" he asked.

Angela shook her head. "I'm not sure, Mr. Ragnall. I just feel I shouldn't go on, not knowing what all this is about."

"What all what is about, Angela?" Ragnall asked.

She looked back over the country they had come across. "The bridge," she said. "Why did you blow it up?"

He moved closer to the buckboard and swept his hat to the back of his head. The moonlight gleamed down on his lean but handsome features. There was a boyishness about him that Angela found attractive. Zeb Ragnall's letters had impressed her with their sincerity and she had been willing, after much personal debate, to give herself to this man offering kindness for the sake of her ailing brother. And when Zeb Ragnall had turned out to be so presentable, she could hardly believe her good fortune.

"I had to blow the bridge," he said. "I've worked hard for what I've got."

"I don't understand," she said. "People must need that bridge to get into and out of Glory Creek. Surely—"

"I gave thought to them, sure," Ragnall answered. "And I feel mighty disturbed for them. It ain't my way to hurt anybody."

"Then why do it, Mr. Ragnall?"

"Be better if you called me Zeb, Angela. But like I said back in Glory Creek, I'm not expecting you to throw yourself at me. We'll give ourselves plenty of time to know each other. Still, we've got to start somewhere, haven't we?"

Angela blushed. Then, clasping her hands on her lap, she said more quietly, "All right, Zeb. But please explain to me about the bridge. I want to understand you, to trust you. And I want so much for this to work out, for my brother's sake."

Zeb Ragnall stared into the night, head tilted to one side as if listening for expected sounds. Finally he spoke:

"Got me a lot of gold stashed away, Angela. I guess when a man gets something for the first time in his life, he just can't keep his mouth shut. He's got to tell somebody, to prove how darned smart he's been." He turned his gaze to her, then his eyes roamed down her body and she felt a sudden urge to cover her bosom with her hands. But then he sighed and glanced away.

"I've been real lonely, Angela. A man heads into the hills, searches, digs, hopes. Maybe twice a year he goes to town and has some comforts. But, for the most of it, it's sleeping on the ground, bustin' up his hands with diggin', and breakin' his back, day after day, in all kinds of weather. Loneliness is about all a man ever gets."

Angela felt sympathy rising within her. "Why did you do it then?"

He smiled shyly at her, then looked away again and his face tightened. "Why? Guess I asked myself that a thousand times in the last five years. But I kept thinking of the day when somethin' would break my way. And one rainy mornin', there it was. My future for the takin'—gold, enough of it for a man to set himself up proper, to get himself somebody to love, to beat off the loneliness with another person who might come to love him one day ..."

Ragnall looked back at Angela and his eyes were moist. "You're beautiful. I didn't have the nerve to tell you that before, but I wanted to. Soon as I met you in your room, I told myself, 'Zeb Ragnall, if you ever done anythin' smart in your life, putting that advertisement in the Cheyenne paper sure was it.'"

He smiled and Angela blushed. When she looked down at her hands, Ragnall went on:

"On the way to the bridge, I kept thinkin' of all the people I told about my gold. And I remembered how many of 'em looked at me like they wanted to slit my guts open. I thought, too, of what you could mean to me, how I could get for you the things you want, how I could help your brother get well again and come out and join us. Lots of things I thought of, just lookin' at you, seein' how well you drove the buggy, how sure of yourself you were. So I decided to blow up the bridge and put all those hardcase jaspers behind me. I couldn't take any risks, not with everything I've worked for right within my reach."

Angela reached out and put her hand on his wrist. "I'm sorry, Zeb. I didn't understand."

He took in a deep breath. "Those men you told me about, Angela—they were after our gold. I had to blow up the bridge—for your sake."

She picked up the reins. Then, with a shy smile, she said, "Shall we go on, Zeb?"

He grinned and pulled his hat back to his forehead. Turning his horse, he let out a whoop of joy, put his horse into a run and led the way off the slope and down into the desert country. He rode in front now so she couldn't see his face, and he was glad that the hoof beats drowned out the laughter which he couldn't control. He liked the look of her. She had spirit, too, and by hell, he'd have her. Once she got a taste of comfortable living, the rest would be easy. But he'd have to be careful not to let her know that while he was checking out the Cheyenne office of the Wells Fargo Company, he'd seen her on the street with her crippled brother. He couldn't let her discover that, even before he had his hands on the gold bullion, he'd decided to have her as his woman.

Zeb Ragnall rode hard into the night, giving only a passing thought to the big man on the black stallion who'd dogged their trail to the bridge. Well, that dodger couldn't follow them now.

Isaac Madie was tired. He was sweating more than he ever had, even in the height of the summer down on his own place. Here the wind was so hot and dry it cracked his skin. But he kept his complaints to himself because his sons watched him as they rode, wondering, he knew, what the hell he was up to.

Isaac Madie had no intention of telling them a single damn thing. So he pushed the big white stallion along, sorry only that he hadn't been able to give the animal more rest in Glory Creek. But things had gone wrong from the very beginning. Ragnall. Miss Grant. Ringo Nyall. Blake Durant. That damned, interfering, nosy lawman. And his boys, making fools of themselves as usual ...

He wiped the sweat off his brow and patted the Bible in his coat pocket. He wondered why such an honest, decent, God-fearing man should suffer so much torment.

Mark and Luke rode at his side but John was still behind the last rise, the wind forcing him to cling desperately to the shallow neck of his bony nag. When John finally reached them his eyes were misty and sweat ran down his terribly lean face. He kept away from his father, still unsure why the old man had kicked the feet from under him in town. But then John had never understood much of what his father did.

"You figurin' to slow us down, boy?" Isaac said sullenly.

John shook his head and worked uncomfortably about in the saddle. "Pa, I come as fast as I could, but you was beltin' along too much for me. My horse, she ain't half—"

"Horse is fine. Broke it in myself when you was scratchin around and snivellin'. You aim to claim, boy, that I don't know how to break a horse proper?"

John's sweat glistened in the moonlight. He looked to his brothers for support but didn't even get a grunt.

"Pa, I wouldn't say nothin' like that. Ain't nothin' you can't do better'n any man alive. It's just—"

"Get ahead, boy—slow down and I'll run right over you. Move, now! We got a killer to find to wring the evil out of." Isaac's fiery glance went to his other two sons. "Same for you two heathens. Keep your mind on the trail and keep thinkin' of only one thing—your brother's killer up front of us, ridin' with the wages of sin in his buckboard and a branded woman sittin' beside him, the scars of her transgressions there for all to see and be disgusted with."

Isaac pushed John in the back and the lean little youth almost fell from the saddle. But with desperate speed he righted himself, aided by the immobility of the slump-backed, frail-legged range poke. Getting the mare into motion, John hurried her along as fast as she could go. Mark and Luke loped along in his wake, with the fiery-eyed Isaac bringing up the rear. Isaac kept mumbling to himself all the way down to the river. Then, when he saw the bridge down and the river running too fast to cross, he sat rigidly in his saddle and pointed an accusing finger at the ground.

"The work of the devil!" he exclaimed.

His sons sat their horses silently behind him, watching the wild torrent rush through the distorted remains of the old bridge. Isaac moved forward, inspecting the ground. The night wind whipped against his broad deep chest but he paid it no heed. His interest was only in the single set of tracks cutting along the muddy bank for several hundred yards before they broke onto firmer ground and headed due north. Halting his stallion, Isaac let out a weary growl and said:

"The buckboard went across and Nyall followed it. But Durant came upon these troubled waters too late. Knowing him for the man he is, we'll take our guidance from him. But when we come upon him, none of us will be fooled by the manners of the man. The greed for gold is in all men not nurtured by the true wisdom of the Good Book. We'll go on."

With that Isaac pushed his horse into a run. For another two hours they rode north. The big man was sweating profusely when he finally drew rein where Durant's tracks led into the river at a narrow section.

Luke said, "Went across here, Pa."

"I can see that, boy. My eyes have been blessed by the Lord to see what they must. Durant is a capable man, but no more so than any of us. The blood of Isaac Madie is in your veins, and don't ever forget it. Mark and Luke will go first."

The two sons looked anxiously at the swift run of the river, then glanced at each other and gulped. But under the scathing look of Isaac they put their horses into the river. The water swirled about them, unseating Mark before he reached midstream. On the river bank, Isaac watched and cursed Satan under his breath as John sweated and went white. John knew he could not disobey his father, and he was certain that he would soon be dead. His heart fluttered as Isaac turned to him and said:

"In with me, boy, and keep high and to my right. Give me due warnin' if there is any debris likely to rip my horse open."

Isaac sent the stallion into the river and John entered the stream some twenty feet higher. The river soon pushed John's weary-legged horse down onto the old man's. Isaac swung wildly at his son. Ahead, Mark and Luke had reached the opposite bank, and now they squatted on the ground, watching Isaac and John cross.

Isaac, holding his Bible high in one hand, pushed John's weight off him with the other. But the river kept the youth's mare planted firmly against the old man's stallion. Isaac knew if his horse went under, he would go down with him. He whipped his huge frame about and was about to deal his son a lusty blow for survival, when his horse floundered on the river bottom, found footing and then lunged forward. John was swept downstream, his horse floating rather than swimming. John dropped off its back and struck out for the bank fifty feet below Mark and Luke, who made no attempt to come to his aid.

The boy's eyes were wide with fright, and all his strength gone when he finally was tumbled onto the bank, to lie there, gasping for breath. His horse came out of the river another twenty feet down.

When John could finally lift his head, his father stood tall before him, his Bible clasped to his huge chest. Mark and Luke, holding the three horses, were up on the edge of the bank. Isaac reached down, plucked his son from the mud and heaved him up the slope of the bank. Letting out terrified grunts, John crawled, slid and gouged his way to firm ground. Isaac came up behind him, pulled him to his knees and then, pushing Mark and Luke down onto their knees, he stood and looked at the starry sky above.

Isaac gave thanks for salvation with the river water running down his legs. His three sons bowed their heads, but once Mark and Luke looked at each other, and grim understanding of something passed between them.

FIVE

NOTHING MEEK

Blake Durant had crossed the river and let Sundown rest for ten minutes before he swung into the saddle again. He looked back across the river to the other bank to see if he was being followed, but the moonlight-soaked prairie was empty. Blake touched heels to Sundown's ribs and the horse took a mighty lunge upwards. Then the black's right leg buckled in a pothole and his shoulder went down. Blake, not yet fully settled, was thrown forward and out of the saddle. His head struck rock. Through a dark haze he saw Sundown struggling to his feet, then blackness claimed him.

Sundown's cold lips were nuzzling him and the sounds of hoof beats matched the throbbing in his head as Blake Durant pushed himself off the wet, rank-smelling ground. He knelt, bowed over, as the wind whipped about him and Sundown nickered. Blake lifted a hand to his head and a heavy drive of pain lanced into his brain.

"When your head is clear, Durant, we'll talk."

Blake stirred himself to full alertness and looked up. John, Mark and Luke were standing beside their horses. Isaac Madie was seated on a deadfall, his Bible on his lap, his white shirt stained with muddy water, his wet clothes clinging to his big frame. His face was expressionless except for a glint of suspicion in his black eyes.

Blake lifted himself erect, went to Sundown and took his canteen from the pommel. He uncorked it, drank, then tipped water over his head. His fingers gingerly felt along his scalp until he found the gash, about an inch long and not very deep. He returned the canteen to the saddle, picked up his hat and palmed the mud off it. Only then did he return his attention to Isaac Madie.

"You might have helped me, done something for me, Madie," he said.

"Might have, and I thought about it, Durant. I also thought about the help you gave me once. But when the devil gets his hooks into a man, he changes. He ain't ever the same, is forever damned."

"Keep that for your boys," Blake said wearily.

Isaac shrugged his huge shoulders. "A man's greed dictates the course of his life, Durant. I think you have the stench of gold in your nostrils."

Blake snorted at him and wiped mud from his clothes. Then he walked down to the river, cleaned his face, washed and wrung out his gold bandanna and replaced it on his neck. After that he pulled Sundown down to the edge of the river and washed him down, bucketing hatfuls of water over him. Sundown, eager to be on the go, drew himself up the bank and eyed Isaac Madie and his three sons warily. Blake followed him and turned the horse so the early sun fell on the cradle of the saddle. Taking his waterproofed tobacco pouch from his pocket, Blake proceeded to make himself a cigarette. All this time Isaac Madie watched him.

Drawing in smoke, Blake said, "Now what the hell's this all about, Madie?"

"About you lookin' for bounty, Durant. I don't want no lies about you bein' worried about that sinner woman who's gone off with a killer. There's forty thousand dollars' worth of gold bullion in this and I believe you have your black heart set on getting it."

74

Blake grinned thinly at him. "That so, mister?"

Isaac nodded grimly and came to his feet. He kissed his Bible and put it in his coat pocket, then he swayed back and forth, his mouth set rigidly and his stare probing Blake's eyes.

"It is so, Durant. One of my boys overhead you talking to Sheriff Lasting before you sneaked out of Glory Creek and got onto the trail of the man named Nyall."

Blake's eyebrows arched. "You know about him, eh?"

"As a disciple of the Lord, Durant, I have access to all kinds of information. Nyall is in fact the man my boys were huntin', not Zeb Ragnall. So we can forget about callin' that murderin' swine by the name of Ragnall from now on, provided there is a 'from now on' for you, Durant."

Blake drew again on the cigarette and let the smoke roll about in his mouth. His body was stiff from the time spent in the mud. And he was hungry. In addition, he was beginning to get impatient with Isaac Madie.

"Get to the point, Madie. You're wasting my time."

Isaac's brows crowded his black eyes. He drew in a deep breath and eyed his sons fiercely as if daring them to interrupt. But they were content to just watch, so Isaac turned to Blake.

"We have time, Durant, and I intend to use it in the service of the Lord. Nyall robbed a Wells Fargo office with the help of my unfortunate son, Matthew. Now, Matthew was not a bad boy. Easily led perhaps, and susceptible to the lying overtures of a man spoken for by Satan. But he was a man who, deep down, loved the Lord, and under my guidance would have become an honorable man. He would have walked the country spreading the gospel as I do myself, and be proud to do it."

Blake blew out smoke. Isaac's eyes narrowed and went hard.

"His death will be avenged, Durant, take my word on that. I cannot let a sinner go unpunished. He will be scourged of his sins, I swear it!"

Blake pushed his hat to the back of his head and settled against Sundown. "We have to catch up with Nyall first, Madie, and all this talking is giving him more time to get away."

"Patience is a Christian virtue, Durant, so I will not be hurried. I have had to live in a world of evil men and the Lord knows I've done my best to help them mend their ways. I've given my life to the service of my Maker, and he has advised me what to do. The bullion my son stole and was murdered to be relieved of, is my property. I will revenge my boy's death, then take that bullion and use it to further the Lord's work."

"What about Wells Fargo?" Blake asked.

Isaac Madie's face went white. "Maggots! Sucking the life blood from poor, honest people. They sow not, neither do they reap. Parasites!" Isaac Madie, warming to the subject, stormed along the top of the bank, shouldering his sons aside and waving his Bible. "A sinister, sin-bloated, drink-crazed thievin' bunch of misguided reprobates, cast off by the Lord and never meant to tread the path of righteousness. Scum!"

Blake shook his head at this and pulled Sundown closer. As he swung into the saddle, Isaac gave a nod and Mark and Luke drew their guns and held them on Blake Durant. Blake eyed them coldly for a moment before he leaned forward in the saddle, drawing the reins tight through his fingers.

"Madie, you're pushing your boys into trouble they won't be able to handle. I'm going on to find Miss Grant and get her away from a jasper who's been feeding her lies. I don't give a damn if you come along or not, but I'm setting my own pace. If you can keep up, well and good. Just don't get any fool notions of delaying me in any way."

Isaac Madie's face darkened and his neck bulged. Mark and Luke stepped away from him, and John, picking at a sore on his wrist, looked fearfully at Durant.

"You'll not get the Lord's gold, Durant!" the big man cried.

"I don't give an owl's hoot about that bullion, Madie. But if I do happen to get my hands on it, I'll see that Wells Fargo learns where to pick it up."

Isaac Madie drew in a deep breath. "You dare to defy me, Durant!"

Blake gave him a thin smile. "Madie, you don't worry me in any way, and neither do your boys. I'm pushing on. Do what you damn like, but keep the hell out of my hair!"

Blake turned Sundown away and let him walk. Looking straight ahead, he ignored the threat of the drawn guns. At the top of the slope, he swung Sundown south and let him pick up pace.

Behind him, Mark Madie said, "Pa, what'll we do?"

Isaac scowled, then bellowed, "Get on your horses, quick! And put up them guns. You'd likely hit me or yourselves if you got to fire them."

Isaac pushed John out of his way and scrambled onto his big white stallion. He glared after Blake Durant, muttering to himself. Mark and Luke were already in their saddles when Isaac hit the white into a run. But John, dodging away from his brothers' horses, lost his footing again and fell on his face. Moaning, he struggled up, caught the reins of the lean range poke and dragged himself into the leather. It took him several attempts to get the poke facing the right way, then he hit it into a run and gave chase. Ahead of him, Blake Durant had settled Sundown into an easy gait and Isaac, Mark and Luke Madie were thundering their mounts in pursuit across the dry country. The dust from the hoofs rose to blind him, but nothing in the world would have made him turn away from the trail blazed by his father.

The sun was high and the wind hot and dry. Angela Grant drove the horses hard, trying to keep Zeb Ragnall in sight as he scouted ahead. The rim before her was broken by several ancient slides, and on the talus-littered slope of one of these, Ragnall had just drawn rein. Angela breathed a deep sigh of relief. Her hands, arms and shoulders ached from the drag of the reins and her skin seemed to be shriveling on her face and neck. Her clothes were stuck to her body and she had never felt so grubby in all her life.

Slowing the buckboard, Angela eased it into the shade of three gray-barked trees and drew up a few yards from Ragnall. When he turned to her, she saw that he was completely unaffected by the heat. In fact, he looked just as cool as he had that same morning, after blowing up the bridge.

"I thought you'd never stop," she said to him and he gave her a wry smile and pointed ahead. Angela's brow furrowed when she saw the bright glare coming off the baked expanse of unbroken flat country.

"Figured it'd be best to rest the horses here and get the cramp out of us," he said. "You bore up real well, Angela."

Angela felt color rise in her face. He had a disarming way of making her feel uncomfortable when he looked so intently at her.

"I feel so worn out," she said, but without the hint of a grumble in the words. "Where exactly are we going, Zeb?"

Ragnall came off his horse and uncinched the saddle. Dropping it in the shade, he ground-hitched the horse and let it walk off in search of feed. He removed the canteen from the saddle-horn and drank, spilling cool water over his hairy chest. Standing there, braced on wide-planted feet, he looked to Angela to be as trim a man as she had ever known. His body seemed to be all muscle and sinew with none of the loose flesh she had seen on so many townsmen in Cheyenne. Now he smiled at her.

"Well, Angela, I reckon we've put the worst behind us. From now on it'll get cooler and even when we get into the desert, I don't think you'll find it too hard travelling."

"Desert?" she asked, troubled again.

"Small stretch. Should hit it just on sundown if we keep up the pace we been going. Don't have to, though, if you feel yourself gettin' tired again. I reckon we gave everybody behind us the slip."

Angela pushed her dank hair from her face and accepted the canteen from him. The heat was like a blanket about her.

She crossed to the first of the trees, sat against the trunk and stretched out her legs. The cramp in her body began to lessen and she smiled with the relief of it.

Ragnall ambled over and sat beside her. He picked up a stick and began to scratch about in the dirt, making circles and putting his initials into them. Angela watched, feeling there was still a lot of youth in him. Then her gaze fell on the initials he kept scratching: R.N.

"What does R.N. mean?"

Ragnall dropped the stick and Angela saw a tightness stretch at his face. He erased the letters with his boot.

"The initials stand for Red Nelson," he said. "He owned the last ranch I worked on before I took to mining."

"Is he still a friend of yours, Zeb?" she asked, hoping to learn a little more about him. She'd always found it profitable to let men talk about themselves.

Ragnall shrugged. "Nelson was all right, I guess. As a bossman he was no worse than all the others."

"You don't like working for other people, do you, Zeb?"

He looked up sharply. "Who does?" he rasped.

She settled back, smoothing her skirt over her knees. "I don't suppose any man really does, Zeb. Is that why you took up mining, to be your own boss, to go where you liked, when you liked?"

"Guess so."

Ragnall rose, stretched his legs and walked about the shaded area lazily. Angela again had the feeling that impatience was gnawing at him, that he was eager to shift on. From time to time she saw him gazing back over the country they had come.

"Zeb, have you ever been lonely, I mean really lonely?"

He turned slowly. "Yeah, I've been lonely, Angela."

"So have I. Sometimes I've been so lonely I could have screamed just to have somebody come up and ask me what was wrong. There have been times in my life when I believed there would never be another happy day for me."

Ragnall came back and squatted in front of her. He reached out and took her hands. "I had it hard for five years. I had it real hard. Even now, with those hard times behind me, I can't forget them. I've been so hungry I scratched the ground for salt, been so thirsty I chewed sticks and kept a pebble in my mouth for days. Some nights I've been so tired I couldn't sleep with the aches in my body. I've been so damned hot, every part of my skin crawled, and so cold I couldn't shift my toes or fingers." He breathed a deep sigh. "A man don't ever forget those times, and it's a lie when they say it makes the good times better. Nothing makes the good times better unless a man has money, plenty of it, to do what he likes."

Angela ran her tongue over her dry lips. She did not know how she felt about this man who was still a stranger to her in so many ways. But she knew she did not dislike him, and she felt that one day perhaps she would have some regard for him. But never real love. She had experienced that once and been hurt by it. She would never really love anybody again.

"I got me a lot of gold, Angela. I took gold dust and traded it in for bullion. With bullion a man can buy in any territory. Everybody values gold bullion, and it holds its price no matter what. Tomorrow morning we'll pick up that bullion and stash it in the buckboard. Then we'll cross the border and head south. We'll buy a place and stock it and settle down to ranching. We're gonna have neighbors and friends callin' by, and we'll have some real high times. That's what you can marry into, Angela, just as soon as you like."

She tried to withdraw her hands but his fingers tightened their hold. Angela was surprised that his hands were so smooth.

"When did you give up hard work, Zeb?" she asked.

He frowned, glanced at his hands and smiled awkwardly. "Just as soon as I could, Angela, months ago now. Nights I used to sit and rub grease into them, wanting to put behind me every reminder of the hard times. And you can see how good that greasin' worked. Now I got me hands as smooth as a card player's, eh?"

Angela nodded, but a wrinkle of concern rose within her. Ragnall pulled her close suddenly and pushed her hair back from her neck. She did not move even when his lips caressed her skin. She felt his other hand sliding up her waist to stop just short of a breast. She stiffened.

Ragnall said, "I figure to have you, Angela, and I can't see how it matters whether it's now or later."

Angela drew back. "No, Zeb, not like this. Not now. Not here."

His stare settled seriously on her. "You came out this way in answer to my letters. I thought your decision had been made, that you wanted to get married, have some money, be able to look after your brother."

She pushed herself to her feet and he rose with her, his body hard against hers. But she twisted free of his grasp and walked off, feeling a strange relief lifting inside her.

Ragnall watched her go, his face creased in a grin. Then he shifted his gunbelt a little higher on his trim waist and began to follow her. Angela walked into the blazing sunlight and the terrific heat once again claimed her. She stopped, looked uncomfortably about her, and heard him come up.

"I don't know, Zeb," she said without turning. "I need time. You're much more of a man than I expected. There— there are many things about you that I like and admire."

Ragnall drew beside her. Then, just as Angela was preparing to ward off his next advance, the warning rattle of a snake froze her. She glanced down and saw a coiled rattler poised to strike.

Ragnall pushed her aside and then his hand flashed for his gun in a blur of speed. The Colt bucked and the bullet separated the rattler's head from its body. Angela staggered back, her face deathly white.

Ragnall watched her for a moment before he walked across to the snake and kicked it away. Returning, he muttered, "A man can be lucky."

His voice brought Angela out of her shocked state. She dropped her hands and looked fearfully at him, shaking her head a little. She saw him in a different way now and remembered a lot of confusing things about him—the way he had met her in Glory Creek, the absolute confidence of the man, his habit of looking back across his shoulder whenever they stopped, the blowing up of the bridge ... his smooth skinned hands. And now there was the way he had drawn his gun and so effectively dealt with the snake. That, she knew, had been the action of a man very much used to guns. Could a miner become so proficient with a handgun, she asked herself?

"Horses should be about right, Angela," he told her and went past her to saddle his horse.

Angela returned to the buckboard and climbed up. She sat very still, looking into the blazing glare of the baked country ahead. Tremors of fear still ran through her body and her mouth was so dry she could hardly swallow. She opened her canteen, drank, and patted some cool water onto the back of her neck. Then, picking up the reins, she kicked the brake off and let the buckboard horses go from the shade and into the blast of heat and sun-glare. She didn't even look at the man called Zeb Ragnall.

SIX

ISAAC'S LOAD

"We'll stop here."

Isaac Madie drew his horse into the shade of the three trees and dropped wearily from the saddle. He took a step away from his horse and his left leg buckled under him. He reached back and grabbed the pommel and stopped himself from falling. Then, his face wet with sweat and raw from the heat and dry wind, he lay against the big stallion's sweat-foamed side and mopped his brow. It was several moments before he could get sufficient breath into his lungs to stand erect. He looked sullenly at Mark and Luke who had come effortlessly out of their saddles and were already looking for a place to stretch out. John Madie was still coming up the barren bench country, his horse short-stepping, and John looking as tuckered out as the bony horse.

Blake Durant had drawn rein but sat on Sundown, watching the old man carefully. He knew that Isaac was at the end of his tether, that the hard, hot ride had reduced him to an exhausted hulk, and there would be no more travelling that day.

"Horse is spent," Isaac told Durant. "Push him further and he could break down completely."

Blake nodded. Isaac limped away from the horse as John came up. Casting a scornful glance at his youngest son, the old man growled:

"See to my horse, boy, then get a fire going. Have them lazy brothers of yours help some instead of wearin' out the seats of their pants."

Isaac strode past Durant, trying to walk normally, but his legs were bowed and he couldn't restrain the grunts that came from him. He rested against a tree, removed his hat, mopped his brow, then dug out his Bible. He stood fanning his face with the Bible, his surly look fixed on Durant again.

Blake looked into the distance for a time before he walked Sundown, leaning to one side of the saddle to inspect the ground. The buckboard tracks were clear in the dust near the trees.

"They're no more than two, three hours ahead, Madie. I'll keep going. Might catch up before the light fails."

Isaac's mouth twisted and his chest heaved. His brows crowded his eyes. "Ain't nobody breakin' outa this camp, Durant. We're all stayin' on. We'll rest up and pull out together in the morning."

Isaac Madie motioned his boys to come closer. Eyeing Durant warily, Mark and Luke drew alongside him. Isaac suddenly reached across and whipped Mark's gun from his holster. He then pushed both his sons back, and said savagely:

"Ain't nobody movin' out till I'm good and ready to go with 'em, Durant. And don't figure to best me later and sneak off in the night, because my boys will be set to watch you. John, get that fire goin' and Mark, you and Luke take the horses up yonder and rope 'em down then sit with 'em. I'll have John bring some grub to you later."

Mark and Luke went off and John was already gathering kindling wood when Blake Durant said, "Madie, don't push me."

"I'll push all I like, mister. I been thinkin' a lot about you on the ride here. What frets me most is why you didn't head on home back east away instead of driftin' down this way. Didn't you tell me you had a place, and a brother workin' for you?"

"I said that, yeah."

"And you mentioned a woman, I seem to recall."

Blake nodded and his face darkened. "There was a woman, once."

Isaac sniggered and wiped sweat from his face with his sleeve. "Once, eh? Got a place and a brother workin' it for you, and you're driftin'. Like I said, I'm still obliged to you for the help you gave when you drifted through my country, Durant. But don't you buck me, mister. My horse is tuckered out and I'm a man who regards my animal in a better light than I regard most folks. Now come down and sit and be sociable."

Blake sucked in his breath and worked out of the saddle. Taking Sundown into the shade, he looped the reins over a low branch, then came back to the old man who was watching John still trying to get a fire going. Finally, losing patience, Isaac planted his boot in the seat of his boy's pants and sent him sprawling. He then knelt down, gathered some dry tinder together and, thumbing a match alight, soon had a fire going. John stayed on the ground looking fearfully at him until Isaac barked:

"Get the pot and the coffee. And don't forget the water, boy! I got to lead you by the nose all my sufferin' life?"

91

John scrabbled to his feet and hurried to where Mark and Luke had halted the horses. Mark threw the black coffee pot at him, and Luke opened a canteen and poured water into it. Then Mark tossed a bag of coffee to his brother and said:

"See if you can get back without spillin' everything, John."

John turned and hurried back to his father who had set thick green sticks crisscrossed to hold the pot. He heaped dry wood under the pot and settled down on his haunches, his black coat dragging in the dust, his heavy-lidded stare fixed on Blake.

"Done your share of prayin', Durant?" he asked.

Blake didn't reply.

"If you ain't before, you better learn to if you're stayin' with me, mister. Prayer is the gate that opens the way to the Lord's domain. You'll walk that path with me, Durant, and I guarantee you'll come to the end of the journey a better man."

Blake settled down out of the fire's smoke and made himself a cigarette. Lighting it from a burning stick, he drew heavily, then returned the stick to the fire and regarded the grizzled face of the old man. Isaac Madie had got the upper hand on him through his own carelessness. Blake had never really taken the old man seriously. Now that he understood him better and saw him as a shrewd old dodger, he decided to give him more respect. As for the talk about goodness and righteousness, Blake wasn't impressed at all. Underneath he saw all the layers of hypocrisy.

Blake waited, smoking, watching the fire and thinking of all the trouble that had come his way since he rode into Glory Creek. Then he turned his mind back to his own country, to his brother working the ranch and waiting for him to return. He went just a little further into the past and thought briefly of Louise Yerby, the woman he had hoped to marry, the love death had stolen from him.

He sighed. The hurt was still there, though deep buried. He wondered how long it would go on, this constant remembering, this pain that came with the smell of a deadwood fire or scent of clean pine, the sparkle of the river, the bunching of clouds, the sight of grass flattened by a sudden squall or leaves flying or a bird circling. It didn't take much to drag him back to the memory of Louise.

"Listen," Isaac said, breaking into Blake's thoughts, "when we come up with that Nyall who murdered my boy, I want you to mind your manners. The Lord gave me Matthew and decreed he should grow up in my image. But that murderin' jasper put an end to that. An eye for an eye ... it's my right to put an end to him."

Blake drew deep on his cigarette and looked into the distance. The wind lifted little dust devils from near the base of the trees. There was no sound but the crackling of the fire and the shuffling of John Madie's boots as he scratched at his leg. Blake lay back, his hat over his eyes. He hadn't succumbed to Isaac's tyranny, but until the old dodger dropped off to sleep he decided he might as well humor him. It was that or beat the stuffing out of him.

Zeb Ragnall led the way across the desert stretch, all the time keeping an eye on Angela Grant. The fact that she had evaded his earlier advances didn't bother him much. There was desert to cross, the gold to dig up and pack into the buckboard, and then there was an easy ride to the border. He would make camp near the little creek where he had stopped on the run down from Cheyenne after killing that damn fool, Matthew Madie. In that camp, with the night about them, he would take Angela, with or without her consent. Then it would be settled and she would be his to do with as he wished.

He rode into the fast-closing twilight and Angela trailed, tired again and eager for a stop at a creek or river where she could wash the dry dust from her skin and perhaps have time to rinse out her clothes. Since seeing Ragnall kill the rattler, her mind had been ticking off the facets of his makeup which didn't sit right with her. She'd had thoughts of turning back to Glory Creek, but she doubted that Ragnall would let her. Blake Durant had been right when he said this wasn't the territory for a woman.

She was frightened now. Ragnall was definitely not a miner who had worked hard and put away an honest fortune. He was too sure of himself, too sharp in his gunplay. As for his clothes, they were a little too fancy—the hand-tooled boots, the lace on the front of his shirt.

Ragnall rode back to her as she was thinking of tying the reins to get a few minutes' sleep. He pointed ahead and called out, "Head for the west side of the rocks. We're out of it now. You can get some rest while I check out the country ahead."

Angela was so bone-weary from the jolting of the buckboard that she merely nodded her head. Just to be rid of the desert's oppressive heat was reward enough at the moment. She turned the buckboard towards the rocks which loomed

95

ahead in the fading light. Ragnall went straight ahead and disappeared into the gloom.

Angela almost fell as she jumped down from the buckboard. She spent some time rubbing the cramp out of her slender thighs before she felt confident enough to go on. She sat on a rock as night closed in. Soon she found herself thinking of Blake Durant, the big, quiet man who had helped her so much and had given her good advice that she had not heeded. She wondered what kind of woman he wanted. There was a deep-seated solemnness about him which must have come from an incident in his past. Had a woman caused it?

Angela suspected it had been a woman. Why was it that all the good men who attracted her were either married or carrying a burn for some other woman? She swept her hair back and sighed wearily. The country about her was flat and dry and the wind was still hot. She felt alone. She had a brother and no other kin. Now she was lost in strange country with a man she had begun to distrust. She sat perfectly still and tears formed in her eyes.

Then Ragnall came back. He was grinning. "Come on, Angela, just a mile or so more and we can dig in for the night, get coffee and beans into us and have a good sleep. It'll be the last time we'll be eating beans, I promise you."

Angela rose stiffly and made her way back to the buckboard. Just one more mile or so. Her body ached for rest.

But she struggled into the seat and took up the reins and with Ragnall leading she let the buckboard swing wide of the clustered rocks. After what seemed ten miles, Ragnall took the reins of one horse and turned the team into a little clearing. He came out of the saddle, hitched the horse and helped Angela down.

"Get comfortable," he said. "Your troubles are over for today."

Then he led the horses behind a clump of trees and moments later she heard the heavy thump of something being loaded into the buckboard.

The bullion. She was confused. Why hadn't he deposited the gold dust in a bank? Other miners used banks. Why turn gold dust into bullion? But once again she was too tired to care. She leaned back and let the night wind, cooler now, sweep across her body.

Ragnall finished loading the bullion into the buckboard in a matter of minutes. Sweating freely, he brought the buckboard back and Angela noticed that the wheels sank deeper into the ground now, leaving tracks that were distinct even in the gloom.

Ragnall unharnessed the horses and turned them out to feed, then made a fire and put coffee and beans on to warm. He kept looking at her all the time, his eyes bright with excitement. While he was busy getting their meal she was safe. Later, if he gave her trouble, perhaps she could distract him somehow and run off and hide. Then, in the morning, she could work out a plan of action. But now she was too weary to even think.

Mark and Luke rode quietly through the night. They had seen the fire's glow from the edge of the desert, and then, using the boulder-strewn slopes for cover, had got to within a hundred yards of the campsite. They saw the man squatted by the fire. A woman was seated at the base of a tree.

Luke Madie said, "It's her all right, and that Nyall jasper. You reckon he's got that bullion yet, Mark?"

"No way of tellin'," Mark sucked his teeth and looked uneasily behind him.

Luke said, "Pa ain't comin'. He'll sleep all damn night."

"If he catches up with us, by hell, he'll come on like a thunderstorm in hell." Mark shuddered at the thought. "Maybe we should go back."

Luke glared at his brother. "He ain't catchin' up with us, so he can go thunderin' where he damn well likes. We got us a hoard of bullion and I ain't lettin' that murderin' scum, Nyall, and his woman keep it. First time in our damn lives we can cuss, chew, talk or do what we like without somebody swattin' us. I ain't goin' back, never, and I ain't worryin' no more about pa. He can go eat his damn good book and I hope he chokes on it."

Mark licked his lips nervously. Although he was as big as Luke, he had never felt obliged to test his strength against his brother. All his life he'd done what Luke wanted to do, unless it went against his father's wishes. The only time he'd ever made a decision for himself was when he was alone with John. He could always tell John what to do. Now he said:

"What do we do, Luke?"

"We kill him, what else?"

Mark swallowed hard. He could see Luke's lean, drawn face clearly despite the night's gloom. The wild look in Luke's eyes unsettled him.

"Just walk up and kill him?"

"Just that. We'll leave the horses here. You go one side of that fire and I'll go on the other."

Mark shook his head doubtfully. "I ain't ... I ain't ever killed nobody, Luke. I ain't like you and Matthew."

"Well, you'd best learn, brother. Just keep thinkin' of what this scum did to Matthew and about the gold he's got, with maybe the woman thrown in. You was eyein' them Glory Creek women real hard afore pa happened along, wasn't you?"

"So were you, Luke."

Luke grinned, drew his gun and checked it. "Ain't denyin' it, Mark. And I'll tell you somethin' else. After we get that bullion and we're clear of pa and this damn country, I'm gonna spend most of every day and night havin' my fun with womenfolk, all kinds of 'em. You hear me, Mark?

I'm cuttin' so far away from pa that I ain't ever gonna do without nothin' again for as long as I live."

Mark mopped his brow with a tattered bandanna and drew in a deep breath. "Okay, then, you go first. But by hell, Luke, you best make sure of him. What I heard of Nyall—"

"What folks'll hear from now on, Mark, is that he's dead."

Luke stepped away from his horse and slipped quietly through the slope brush. Getting to within twenty yards of the fire, he saw Ringo Nyall hunched over the flames. The woman stirred and her eyes gleamed as she looked at Nyall. Luke had the impression that she was worried about something. The smell of beans and coffee drifted across to him. He took a firmer grip on his gun and moved left, towards thicker brush.

Zeb Ragnall walked around the fire and stopped short of Angela Grant. He handed her the coffee pot and said:

"Pour some, real natural like, and sit right where you are. Don't say anything and don't move."

Angela took the coffee pot and stared curiously as his right hand slid down and tipped his coat flap back a fraction. She saw his fingers take hold of his gun. Then Ragnall whirled and went into a crouch. The gun bucked in his hand and she saw brush shake to the impact of two bullets. Then he turned again and the gun bucked two more times. Angela heard a man grunt, then a tall, lean man came staggering out of the brush. He went to his knees, fired a shot into the ground, then pitched forward on his face. He did not move.

Zeb Ragnall straightened, his eyes cold, his features taut. Angela dropped the coffee pot and stepped away from him, her face filled with horror. He shouted:

"You in there! If you ain't dead, come on out!"

There was no answer. Ragnall glanced at Angela and saw the terror in her eyes. He grinned.

"Tried to creep up on us, Angie, girl."

Then he moved forward, the gun ready at his waist.

When he reached the brush, he parted it with one boot, then he reached down, pulled a body clear and pitched it near the fire. Angela lifted a hand to her mouth to stifle a scream.

Ragnall turned the body over with his boot, then he walked to the second. Looking up, he said, "Madie boys."

Angela couldn't take her eyes from the dead men. She remembered them as two of the three who had threatened her in Glory Creek. A shudder went through her.

Ragnall stepped over the bodies and approached her. Angela backed away, shaking her head wildly. Ragnall came on, holstering his gun and still grinning.

"No!" Angela called out, then she turned and broke into a run.

She was near the buckboard when Ragnall caught up with her. He grabbed her by the arm and flung her into the side of the buckboard. Angela's fear of him consumed her now.

"No, please!" she screamed.

He laughed. "Ma'am, I think it's time you learned a few things. To start with, you've got to know who runs this outfit."

Angela slapped his face. Ragnall grabbed her wrist, drove her hard back against the buckboard and back-handed her to the face. Angela let out a cry of fear and he hit her again.

"You're a murderer!" she screamed. "You gave them no chance. You didn't know what they wanted. You didn't wait!"

"What they wanted was my gold, ma'am," Ragnall said and when Angela kicked at his shins he slapped her four more times.

Angela's vision clouded. "You're nothing but a swine!" she whimpered.

Ragnall grimaced and tore her blouse away. Angela butted at him, then tried to sink her teeth into his face. Completely enraged now, and tasting blood in his mouth, Ragnall drew back his hand and slammed it hard against her jaw. Angela sagged at the knees and he swung her away. She hit the ground and rolled, her skirt flying up over her head. Ragnall wiped his bloody mouth on his sleeve. The glow from the fire played on Angela's naked thighs and full, firm breasts.

He stood there for a long time, looking down at her, pleased with what he saw. Then he returned to the fire and refilled the coffee pot. Waiting for it to come to the boil, he crossed to where Luke and Mark Madie lay dead.

A bitter curse came from him, then he followed their tracks back to where their horses were tied. He ran his hand over them; they were still warm. So they had come at a dead run. Ragnall climbed the slope and peered into the darkness. Silence and emptiness met his gaze.

He refilled his gun and went back to the fire where he poured himself a mug of coffee and studied Angela again before he kicked dust over the ashes. Then coffee mug in hand, he stood against the buckboard and stared thoughtfully into the distance.

SEVEN

"VENGEANCE IS MINE ..."

Isaac Madie awoke with, a start and glared furiously about him. It was too quiet, he thought. John was huddled in a ball, and the trussed Blake Durant was watching him sourly.

Isaac stretched his arms above his head. The night's rest had completely restored his energy and strength. He felt he could take on a legion of devils single-handed.

Moving across to John, he drove his boot into the boy's bony ribs. John jumped to his feet, waving his hands wildly before he came completely awake. Isaac snorted at John's antics, "Get your brothers back here. Horses should be rested enough. We'll push on, eat on the way."

John dug sleep out of his eyes and wiped his still running nose on his sleeve. Then he broke into a stumbling run up the rise and opened his mouth to call to his brothers. He came to an abrupt halt when he found the clearing empty and Mark and Luke's horses gone. After looking anxiously around, John finally ran back to his father.

"Pa ... they're gone—they're gone! Mark and Luke ... they ain't where they was."

A curse rumbled from Isaac Madie. He thundered up the slope to look for himself, John trailing.

"Musta gone off for a ride," John said.

Isaac whirled around. "Damned idiot!" He pitched John down the slope, then he inspected the ground to read the signs. Rising he shook a ham of a fist in the air.

"Seed of the devil! Damnable scurvy scum!"

John stood off, brushing the dust from his tattered levis. He had one foot planted on his battered range hat and his long hair was dust-choked and untidy about his narrow shoulders. He studied his father anxiously, waiting for the next outburst.

But Isaac quickly gained control of himself and strode to where Blake Durant was roped to the trunk of a tree. He cut him loose, walked to his horse and hurled the saddle on its back. Then, hearing Durant move across the hard ground behind him he said:

"My two boys are bewitched by the devil's gold. By all that's good in me, I'll catch up with them and do what I must!"

Blake worked the cramp from his limbs and saddled Sundown. He wanted to step up to Madie and hammer at the man's granite-like jaw. But, gunless, he was in no mind to pit himself against the hot-tempered lunatic.

As John labored to get a saddle over his bony range poke, Blake said, "Do I get my gun, Madie?"

"Nope, mister, you do not." Isaac produced his Bible and brandished it at Durant. "That's the only weapon any of us need. You'll see—I'll make those scum crawl on their bellies beggin' for mercy. I'll make them cringe and pray for forgiveness till their knees wear away. I'll thrash the evil out of them if it kills me and them!"

"Which won't take care of Ringo Nyall," Blake said. "The way I see it, John there is worse than useless in a scrape. That leaves you—one man against two double-crossing sons out to beat you to the gold, plus a notorious gunfighter who'll blast you from the saddle as quick as a blink."

Isaac studied Blake for a long time, grunted in decision. "When the time comes, I'll return your gun, Durant. Until then, shut down. Nobody else is going to take the devil's side against me. Nobody."

John had finally cinched the saddle and was sitting his horse. He wiped at his nose and worked across to his father's side. Smiling uncertainly at the big man, he muttered, "I didn't ride off, Pa, did I? I stayed with you."

Isaac scowled at him. "Get ahead. You see anybody, give us warning."

"Sure, Pa, sure." John hit the poke into an awkward run and Blake drew alongside the big Bible-puncher.

"Madie, ever since I've known you I've had the feeling that most of what you say is gibberish. Now I'm positive of it."

Isaac eyed him angrily. "Ain't nobody asked for your opinion."

"Nevertheless you're getting it. All your damned preaching is a front for what you really are, a cover for what you're really after. Gold, Madie. Gold!"

"Damn lie, Durant! I got no love for gold—but I know what good I can do with it. I can build me a church and rake in the sinners and teach them the right way of life. And I can get my boys to serve with me. I'll spread the gospel to the four corners of this territory and the wrath of the

Lord will strike down the fools who try to stop me. Which includes you, Durant."

"You won't get away with it, Madie."

Isaac's eyes almost disappeared under the flabby flesh of his cheekbones. "Who'll stop me, mister?"

"I will."

Isaac glowered for a moment, then he sat tall and roared with laughter. His whole body shook and the tears rolled from his eyes.

"You, mister? You, a damned back-handin' drifter, with lies thick in your head and a taste for nothin' but the comforts of life? You, Durant, are gonna stop me?"

Blake turned his horse up the slope, saying, "It gets harder and hotter from here on, Madie. I'd keep a rein on my energy if I were you."

With that, Blake rode on. As he topped a rise he saw John Madie ahead, a forlorn, derelict figure. Blake put Sundown into an easy gait, meaning to nurse him now because he was positive that just ahead there was the kind of trouble only a quick gun and a fast horse might get him out of.

Zeb Ragnall pulled Angela Grant from the ground where she had huddled in fear of him during the night. In dawn's first gray light she could see the set of Ragnall's face. She remembered how he had so effectively killed the rattler and then had cut down the Madie brothers. He was no miner; he was a man who lived by the gun. And she was sure he'd killed before, perhaps often.

Ragnall pushed her towards the buckboard. She tidied her skirt and tried to hold her torn blouse across her bosom. Ragnall stood back and watched her, grinning thinly. When he came forward to help her into the buckboard she stepped away from him.

"Don't touch me."

Ragnall's smile went crooked. His look went to her bosom and Angela felt the heat rise in her face. Suddenly all the trouble of the night before came rushing back into her mind.

She gasped, "You—you didn't! You couldn't have!"

Ragnall chuckled. "No, ma'am. Ain't my way to take a woman who don't know what's happenin' to her. But I'll have you, Angie, girl, when I'm good and ready. And it won't be a case of takin' you, either. There'll be some givin' comin' from you."

Angela's upper lip peeled back. "I'll kill myself first!"

"Suit yourself, ma'am. But for now, get into that seat and start drivin'. We had two visitors last night and I reckon we might have some more today. Only we ain't goin' to be sittin' about waitin' for 'em."

Angela saw his face go tight and fear churned at her again. She stepped up to the buckboard seat. The horses were already harnessed. She took up the reins and glanced back at the buckboard bed where burlap covered the gold bullion.

Ragnall rose into the saddle and pointed ahead. "You got a weight in back, Angela, so take care where you drive. You mess it up, woman, and by hell you'll find out something about me that will take the curl outa your hair. Get along now and don't give me any trouble."

Angela flicked the reins and the horses lunged into their collars. The buckboard flooring creaked as the wheels began to roll. Angela worked the horses off the small clearing and headed them for the rolling plains. As far as she could see, the country was flat and barren, hardly any different from the desert stretch they had come through the day before.

But the wind was cool and as yet there was no heat in the day.

For three hours they headed due south, with the black hills in the distance not seeming to get any closer. Then Ragnall directed her to veer to the right.

"Easier going there, but watch out for rocks. This buckboard you bought with my money ain't exactly the best I've ever seen."

Angela ignored his complaint. He led the way for awhile and stopped to direct her between two huge boulders. When she went ahead of him, he rode onto a rise and peered back into the heat-hazed distance. There was no sign of pursuit. Angela slowed the buckboard horses as the terrain became rougher, but she almost fell from her perch when the right side wheel smashed into a rock, bounced high and came down with a thud. The load in the back of the buckboard shifted and pounded down heavily. There was a sharp crack and Ragnall came riding up, his face flushed with anger.

"Damn you, I said to watch it!"

"I can't see everything. If you're so worried, why don't you drive?"

Ragnall waved her to proceed. When the buckboard was running again, he rode at its side, staring anxiously at the front wheel on his side. A curse came from him. He hit his mount into a run and grabbed at the reins and pulled the horses to a stop. Then he wheeled on Angela.

"Damn you, get down! You lost a collar pin. Wheel's wobblin'."

Angela looked calmly at him. "Too bad."

Ragnall's face went white. He reached out and pulled her from the seat. As her feet hit the ground, he swung out of the saddle and shoved her roughly towards the horses. "Hold them steady."

He went down on his knees and inspected the wheel closely. Rising finally, he looked back along their trail. The wheels had dug deep into the softer ground. He drew his gun and went back to the rock the wheel had hit. Looking about, he muttered obscenities until he found the steel pin. He picked it up, dusted it off and walked back. Giving Angela Grant a venomous look, he inserted the pin into the wheel collar and hammered it home with his gun butt. Having done that he grabbed the wheel and shook it roughly. The wheel wobbled. He swore.

Wiping sweat off his brow and glancing back to the trail over which they had come, he said, "Might hold. Now get back up and keep goin', but slow. If you hit anythin' else and bust that wheel again, by hell you'll regret the day you ever read a letter of mine."

"I already regret it," Angela snapped at him. "I've never regretted anything more in my whole life."

Ragnall bared his teeth. "Ma'am, you ain't even started to feel sorrow, I'm tellin' you that for sure."

Angela glared at him and walked to the other side of the buckboard. Climbing back into the seat, she picked up the rein. When the buckboard started to move again, Ragnall took his position beside the wobbling wheel. His lips were tight and his eyes were filled with viciousness as he watched the wheel wobbling badly.

"Slower, damn you, real slow! We got only ten miles to go and we can make it only if you're damned careful."

Angela slowed the horses. She was thinking of the two men who had tried to surprise Ragnall the previous night. Back in town they had always been in the company of their brother. So perhaps he was close by, or somebody else might be trailing them. She pushed back her hair to let the morning wind touch at her neck. If she hadn't been with Zeb Ragnall, she might have found this warm day very much to her liking. But she was with him, and saw no likelihood of escaping him. Even if someone were trailing, there was the danger of Ragnall's quick, accurate gun.

"Lookee there, Pa!"

John Madie drew rein and pointed at the wheel tracks and hoof prints in the soft ground. Isaac moved alongside him, his eyes slitted in concentration. Blake Durant, still waiting for an opportunity to jump the big man, came up with him. Isaac turned to Blake.

"Got it, looks like."

"No doubt," Blake said. "Those wheels are digging deeper. Now you know who has what and where they're headed. What about my gun?"

"Later, mister, when I'm good and ready." Isaac lifted a hand to shield his eyes and peered into the heat-choked distance. There was no sign of dust. Nothing moved. "Still time." He turned to John. "Boy, get up on that rise and try to see somethin'. Hurry now."

John rode off furiously, glad to serve his father. He had discovered that Isaac Madie treated him a whole lot better when Mark and Luke weren't about. Topping the rise, John shaded his eyes and squinted. But he couldn't see anything but the shimmering heat haze. He squinted harder and sat there, as rigid as a pole until his father's angry bellow reached up to him:

"Damn you, boy, don't go to sleep up there! Is there anythin' or not?"

"Nope, Pa. Can't see nothin'!"

"Then get on down!"

John rode back sheepishly, confused at his father's returning anger. He didn't know what he had done wrong this time. He worked closer to Blake Durant and studied his tanned face. Durant was a quiet man, the kind John liked.

Isaac said, "Well, anyway, we can trail them real easy now. What with that buckboard loaded down and the wheels cuttin' deep, they ain't gonna move at no great pace. How far ahead do you reckon them to be, Durant?"

Blake checked the tracks again. "Maybe two hours."

Isaac beamed. "That all, eh? Hell, we'll be up on them come noon."

"Maybe," Blake said. He was watching other tracks winding off the trail towards a small clearing just ahead. He let Sundown pick his way along while Isaac Madie stopped dead when he reached the rim of brush around the clearing. The two bodies lying under the wash of the sun were covered with a light gray dust, proof that they had been in that position for many hours.

Blake was coming out of the saddle when Isaac Madie rode up. The old man's gaping mouth closed with a snap when he saw the dead men. He jumped from the saddle and let his horse run. Down on his knees, he lifted Mark's head. All color drained from his face. He shook his son's head, desperately seeking a spark of life. But Mark's lifeless eyes stared at nothing.

Isaac lowered his son's head gently, then he reached out to turn Luke's face from the dust. A deep groan came from him. John had ridden up and now he watched his father with growing concern.

"Pa?"

"They're dead, boy, shot down by an agent of the devil!"

John shook his head in disbelief. Blake Durant looked on, taking note of the sincere grief of the old man. For the first time he felt sympathy for him. John jumped from his horse and stood beside his father, who kept looking up at the sky as tears coursed down his cheeks.

Blake Durant swung out of the saddle, hitched Sundown, and walked back into the brush. He picked up a Winchester and checked it. The rifle had not been fired. Walking along the tracks left by a man on foot, he came to where Mark had met his death. Blake saw the burned brush, the trampled section, a strip of shirt caught on a branch. From the signs on the ground he worked out that whoever had killed them had dragged both from the brush into the clearing.

Isaac was looking down now, his chest heaving, his face white. John stood beside him, peering stupidly into his face.

"Pa?"

"Be quiet, boy!" Isaac said, and his voice was almost gentle.

Blake Durant searched around for soft ground and began to dig with his saddle spade. Sweat ran down his body but he was glad to have something to do to keep him away from the broken hulk of the old man, Isaac Madie.

Blake outlined a hole big enough to hold both Madie boys' bodies and was deepening it when Isaac came and knelt beside him. The old man put his Bible down and began to claw at the ground with his bare hands. Blake saw a fingernail tear and blood begin to flow, but the old man continued to work, no sound coming from him, no expression on his shocked face. When the grave was deep enough, Isaac rose and with John's help carried Mark's body there and laid it gently to rest. Then they went to get Luke's body. When his sons were side by side, Isaac dusted his hands on his black silk coat. Then he picked up his Bible and thumbed through the pages until he found the page he wanted. He lifted the book and once more tears rolled down his face.

Isaac's lips moved in silent prayer for many minutes, then he pressed his lips together and tenderly placed the Bible across the joined hands of his sons and started to kick the earth over them. Blake Durant helped with his spade and John filled in the top of the grave, using his battered old hat as a bucket. When the earth had been pounded hard and covered with rocks, Isaac Madie went back to his horse and drew in a ragged breath.

Turning finally to Blake Durant, he handed him his gun without a word. Later, riding across the bench country in the dead middle of the buckboard tracks, Isaac Madie dedicated his life to vengeance.

EIGHT

"HEATHEN!"

Angela Grant's head began to roll about on her shoulders. The heat was drawing the last of her energy. They had not stopped the whole morning, and Ragnall had kept up a non-stop barrage of threats and orders. But she had long since closed her ears to his abuse and now she tried to blank her mind to the pain growing in her body.

The weary buckboard horses plodded spiritlessly through the thick dust. The hills ahead loomed black and uninviting. Angela couldn't see a way through them. But she was positive that Zeb Ragnall knew what he was doing.

It was dead on noon when Ragnall, sweating heavily and looking worried, rode to the top of a small hill. Angela drew rein and slumped forward, letting the reins fall slack. The horses came to a stop.

Ragnall came out of the saddle and kept his horse down below the line of the hill. He went forward on his hands and knees, his gun lifted just out of the dust. Only his hat and forehead showed over the rimline as he checked the country behind. Suddenly he flattened himself to the ground, dragged himself back, then scrambled to his horse in a crouch. In the saddle, his head turned and his eyes raked the terrain. Finally he pointed to heavy brush.

"We'll put the horses in there. By hell, make a noise and I'll kill you, woman!"

Angela didn't know what was going on and she was too weary and weather-burned to argue. She held Ragnall's horse while he unharnessed the buckboard horses and drew them off. Hitching them in cover, he grabbed his own horse from Angela and tied it beside the pair. Then he grabbed Angela by the shoulder and pushed her towards the buckboard.

"Get in and stay down!"

Angela hesitated, recognizing fear in him now. "What is it?" she asked.

"Forget about what it is, damn you, and move! They're comin' fast."

They! Angela backed away from him. This was her chance, perhaps the only chance she would ever have. She turned to run but Zeb Ragnall was too quick. He grabbed her, lifted her over the side of the buckboard, then pushed her legs in. He scrambled into the buckboard bed beside her and pushed her head down to the flooring. Angela could feel hard objects under her legs. The bullion. She lay completely still, wondering and hoping.

A stench came from Ragnall which Angela knew was the smell of fear. She calculated that her chances of getting out of this mess were now about as good as they were ever likely to be.

"Why don't you let me go?" she asked him. "I've done you no harm."

"Done me no good either, damn you, breakin' that wheel on me. Without that we'd be through the hills now and on the way to the border."

"It wasn't my fault," she protested, hoping to distract him, force him into an error.

"No matter whose damn fault it was. Ain't nobody gonna tie down Ringo Nyall. Nobody!"

"Ringo Nyall?"

"That's me, Angie, girl. Maybe you saw the name on wanted dodgers or in the paper?"

"Who is Zeb Ragnall? Did you kill him, rob him?"

Ringo Nyall laughed. "Ain't ever been a Ragnall woman. It's just a name that I figured might belong to a miner, that's all. First time I seen you in Cheyenne with that cripple limpin' along beside you, I figured to have you one day. I made some inquiries and found out all I wanted to know about you—a man runnin' out on you, folks dead and that loco brother of yours dependin' on you. The rest was easy. You took to it like a fish to bait."

Angela let out a deep groan. "You swine. You'd even use a woman's—"

"I'd use anythin', ma'am. Always have, always will. Now shut down because I got some concentratin' to do. I also got me some killin' to do—that fool Isaac Madie, his idiot boy, and that big man on the black folks in Glory Creek took for me. Be a pity to kill him though—he sure took a lot of weight off my shoulders in that fool town."

"Mr. Durant," Angela breathed. "Is—is he coming?"

"I guess he is." Ragnall glanced at her and frowned. "Sounds like you got some feelin' for him. How come?"

Angela shook her head. "I hardly know him. But he helped me. Why should you want to kill him, or anyone? Will your killing never stop?"

123

"They stretch your neck for one killing just as much as they do for four or five or ten. As to why I should kill this Durant and them others, that's about the simplest thing a man ever had to answer." Nyall thumped the sacks behind him with his boot. "For that, Miss Angela Grant. For the bullion. Now why the blazes do you think those two Madie boys came after me last night unless it was to get their thievin' hands on my gold? The same goes for Durant and Isaac Madie and his dim-witted son."

Angela was suddenly cold despite the sun burning down on her. Pressed flat, she could hardly breathe without taking in dust from the flooring. She bit her lower lip and waited, frightened and lonely, fighting to get her mind working on a plan to escape from this cold-eyed killer.

They were in the heart of the open stretch when Isaac Madie's horse faltered under him. Isaac reined up and rubbed the stallion's shoulder, but the horse did not move on. It stood, head down on its chest, sides heaving with exhaustion. Isaac slipped from the saddle. John and Blake Durant slowed their mounts, turned them and came back to him.

Isaac patted the horse's nose and then he pulled his canteen from the saddle. His face was red and sweat ran down his face and neck. His black coat was white-caked with his body's salts.

"Spent," he said to Blake. "Guess I'm too much weight for him."

Blake examined the horse and nodded in agreement. "Best walk him."

"No time," Isaac said.

"It's that or leave him here."

John dropped to the . ground beside his father and extended the reins of his mare. "She ain't much, Pa, but she's better'n she looks. Keeps goin'."

Isaac Madie's eyes clouded thoughtfully. He looked at John steadily for some time before he reached out and patted his head. "No, boy, you keep your horse. It's the only thing I reckon you ever really had for your own. I'll walk and I won't get too far behind. In fact, I don't reckon I got to walk too far now."

John turned his horse and broke into a walk beside his father, leading both horses behind him. He tripped once, wiped his nose with his sleeve and then picked at a sore on his chin. But Isaac Madie was oblivious to his actions. Blake sent Sundown into a fast canter and quickly covered the open stretch. Then he worked Sundown into tree shade and stared ahead. He stiffened in the saddle, frowning, when he saw the buckboard standing in the open, the horses gone from the shafts. There was no sign of anybody.

Blake remained there for a long time, watching, knowing enough about Ringo Nyall to be wary. Without the buckboard, Nyall couldn't carry all the gold bullion with him. Not far or fast, anyhow. And he doubted that the killer would ride off and leave it behind.

He turned Sundown, rode back to Isaac Madie and informed him of what lay ahead. Isaac came to a halt.

"Nobody there?"

"I didn't say that," Blake told him.

"You said the buckboard was—"

"I said I didn't see anybody. Maybe something happened to the horses but we can't find that out here. My advice to you is to take it easy for awhile."

Isaac Madie glared furiously at him. "We just buried my boys—my flesh and blood, Durant! Maybe they weren't all that honest, but there's worse than them masqueradin' as good folks in banks, jailhouses and on court benches, believe me. They strayed from the path of righteousness and turned a deaf ear to my instructions, but I say they were more good than bad."

"Maybe, Madie, but walking straight into drygulch gunfire won't do you or them any good."

Isaac mumbled to himself and John said eagerly, "Pa, I can go look for you. I can sneak in real quiet. Won't nobody see me. I won't—"

"No!" Isaac pushed John away and looked at Blake. "What do you suggest, Durant?"

"That I ride in and draw Nyall's fire if he's still there."

"And lay claim to the gold if it's been left behind? You take me for a fool?"

"I take you for a money-hungry jasper if you don't listen to me, Madie. Nyall's a killer and he's got that girl with him. He won't be taking any chances."

"You said the horses were gone. Why in hell would he do that?"

"To fool us. We've made up over an hour and a half on him by my reckoning. So he would have had half an hour to set himself up. That's time enough to unharness his horses, put them in hiding and   "

"In hiding? Where, damn you? What are you up to, mister?"

"Beyond the buckboard, Madie, is brush heavy enough to hide a half-dozen horses."

Isaac Madie mopped his brow and planted his feet wide. He looked up solemnly at the clear, cloudless sky and seemed to be debating with himself. Then he said:

"Okay, Durant, you go on in. But I'm warnin' you— take off with that gold and so help me I'll hunt you for the rest of my life. I'll put the curse of the Lord on you and be a scourge to you every waking hour of your days."

Blake nodded easily. "Just keep as close behind as you can. If there's a shot, hit the ground and stay there."

Isaac Madie said nothing. Lips pinched tight, he moved ahead of John, leaving his son to drag the two unwilling horses in his wake. Blake let Sundown have his head and gradually drew ahead. He continued on in a straight line for the buckboard, keeping the sun across his left shoulder, when a sudden shout from the buckboard made him wheel Sundown. The fiery black responded immediately and after almost going down in the turn, the big horse lunged on. A rifle shot whipped past Blake's head, and he went down on Sundown's neck and headed for the brush.

Angela Grant, recognizing Blake Durant and his big black stallion, waited for him to get within a hundred yards of the buckboard before she suddenly rose to her knees and shouted at the top of her voice:

"No, Mr. Durant, no!"

Ringo Nyall grabbed Angela's arm and slammed her down. When she struggled to rise he smashed his palm into the back of her neck. Angela's chin hit the boards and an explosion erupted in her head. Groaning, she flattened on the floor of the buckboard and lay still.

Ringo Nyall lifted his rifle to his shoulder and fired off a shot. But by then Durant had wheeled his black and was heading for the brush. Nyall peered into the shimmers of heat rising from the ground between him and Durant, then his attention was drawn away. Coming at the run, hands waving wildly and coat flapping behind him, was the mountain of a man, Isaac Madie.

Directly behind Madie was his son, John, stumbling, falling, rising, calling anxiously to his father to wait. But Isaac Madie had eyes only for the buckboard before him and for the man kneeling in it, a smoking rifle in his hand.

129

Isaac, hair flying wild and saliva running from his lips, cried out, "You're the devil, Nyall, the scum of the earth, the accursed offspring of Satan!"

Ringo Nyall took careful aim and punched off another shot. Isaac Madie came to a sudden halt and his hands dropped to his sides. He looked down at his shirt and the spreading stain of blood. A vicious curse came out of him. John rushed to his side.

"Pa, Pa, you're shot!"

Isaac swept him aside and John went down and stayed down, legs doubled under his scrawny body, eyes fearfully regarding his father. Isaac Madie, gritting his teeth against the pain in his chest, pounded on again. He managed to get his hands halfway up and began to shout again.

"You can't stop an agent of the Lord, Nyall! The Lord has appointed me to act for Him, to rid the world of all sinners, to cleanse the minds of the wicked, to wash the evil from the offenders of this world."

Nyall spat out a curse and lifted his rifle again. This time, believing his last shot must have been wide of Madie, he took more careful aim and gently squeezed the trigger. Isaac Madie stumbled to a halt and stood with his feet braced wide, his chest heaving and blood pumping out of a hole in his chest. John crawled along behind him, keeping his head close to the ground, frightened of being shot himself, but unable to stop from following his father. For John Madie, there was only one man in the world, only one love.

Isaac placed a hand against his chest and watched the blood flow through his fingers. His face was white with pain. He drew in a deep breath. "The ways of the Lord," he intoned, "are difficult to understand."

Then he drew himself to full height and started to drag himself forward. This time he kept both hands on his chest and his lips moved in prayer. He was within twenty yards of the buckboard now and he could see Nyall's face peering at him. Isaac spat out blood and lifted his head defiantly.

"Scum!" he screeched. "Bred in the filth and stench of degradation, damned at birth and exiled and forsaken by the Lord!"

Nyall hastily reloaded the rifle and wiped sweat off his brow. He could see the big man's shirt, shiny with blood. How he stayed on his feet he did not know. He lifted the rifle again and had to wipe sweat from his eyes to see the big man clearly.

"To the devil with his devil's gold!" Isaac Madie roared. "Damn you, Madie!" Nyall shouted, and then he fired his third shot into the big man. The impact knocked Isaac Madie to his knees, but he refused to fall to his face. Kneeling, he swayed from side to side, his face distorted by the savage pain which worked through his body.

"I heed not the words of he with Satan in his mind, Nyall. My spittle will cleanse your soul, black as it is. The wise and the good shall inherit glory. Shame shall be the only reward of the wicked!"

Nyall rose and blasted away at Isaac Madie, who had scrambled halfway to his feet when Nyall's next shots ripped into him, spinning him about. He staggered to the side, straightened, came on a step, then stumbled crazily.

On the ground behind Isaac, John whimpered like a puppy. Tears rolled down his sunken cheeks and all he could see was the swaying, jerking hulk of his father's body.

Isaac drove himself towards the haze-obscured buckboard. He reached out with both hands and his blood dripped onto the ground before him. He was within ten yards of the buckboard when his knees finally gave way under him. He hit the ground with a thud but managed to lift his head.

His eyes were steamy with pain when he croaked out:

"Forgive them not, I beseech Thee, Lord, for they do know what they do!"

Nyall's last shot smashed Isaac's head wide open and he fell, clawing at the ground.

NINE

DAY OF RECKONING

Blake Durant swung down from Sundown and dropped behind a rock. Hearing a shot, he waited for the rush of the slug through the brush nearby. When it didn't come he lifted his head and saw Isaac Madie walking defiantly towards the buckboard, waving his hands and calling on the Lord to help him.

Blake could see no way he could help Isaac now and he crouched there, helpless, too worried about Angela Grant to risk a shot even if he were within side gun range of Nyall. He saw the bullets pour into old Isaac Madie, saw him stagger and finally wilt under the weight of his wounds. But admiration for the old man rose inside Blake Durant. He had seen many men die, but never in his life had he seen the likes of this man's blind courage.

Madie went on and on, seemingly indestructible until the end came, swiftly, brutally. Blake caught up Sundown's reins and began to circle about the brush, hoping to get between the buckboard and the hills. That way he would be positioned to get Nyall. He moved quietly, hearing the echoes of the rifle shots die in the noon stillness.

Angela Grant wiped blood from her mouth and looked fiercely at Ringo Nyall. She saw kill lust in his eyes and was jolted by the gunfire roaring in her ears. But she saw fear rise in his face and her own terror of the man suddenly diminished. She reached out and grabbed for the rifle. Nyall jerked the Winchester free and swung it at her, the butt catching her behind the ear. Angela fell back across the bullion and lay still.

Nyall stared across the clearing towards the brush where Durant had disappeared. Isaac Madie had completely ruined his ambush. With better luck he would have got Durant, had the girl not shouted a warning, then old Isaac Madie would have been easy prey. What John Madie was doing he had no idea nor did he care. One bullet would rip the little runt in half.

Nyall eased himself over the buckboard's side and sprinted towards the clearing where the horses stood, stomping nervously. Nyall dragged the buckboard horses out and quickly harnessed them between the shafts. Then he ran back and tied his own horse behind the buckboard. Angela Grant was still unconscious, a lump showing behind her ear. Nyall felt for a heartbeat and, finding one, decided to take her along. Maybe he could use her.

He climbed into the seat and was about to whip the horses into a run when John Madie jumped up from the ground and came in a weaving, dodging run for the back of the buckboard.

John, having crawled to his father's' side, had lain quiet, unable to believe that his father was dead. He had kissed the tears and blood from the old man's wrinkled face and then Isaac's eyes had opened. Grasping John's skinny shoulder, the old man had pulled him close and whispered:

"Boy, get him! He's the devil's pawn and will damn the world if you let him live. Get him, boy, for your pa!"

Now John was running, tears of grief on his sallow cheeks. He could still see his father's butchered body, could hear the whine of his dying breath within his massive chest. But he could also see the man clambering into the buckboard's driving seat.

John ran fast, his feet no longer awkward. He had his gun in his hand but he couldn't make himself shoot. He had never fired a gun, not even in practice, like Matthew, Mark and Luke were always doing. There was so much he didn't know and he realized he was stupid.

He was rapidly closing in on the buckboard when suddenly Nyall turned and lifted his gun. John jerked his own gun up and fired, then he watched Nyall desperately. His face lit up as he saw Nyall fall to the side and then tumble from the buckboard. John jumped triumphantly into the air and pounded his chest with his gun. The blows hurt but he didn't care.

He had killed Ringo Nyall—he, John Madie, Isaac Madie's youngest son!

John finally stopped jumping. He turned and broke into a run, back to his father. He was almost to him when Nyall rose from the ground, lifted his rifle and aimed it at the running youth's back. He punched off a shot.

John felt the blast hit his spine. He was thrown forward several feet before he fell to the ground. He lay there for a moment, almost within reach of his father's outstretched hand. He saw his father's stare fixed on him, saw the old man's bloodied lips moving.

"Did it, Pa," he croaked. "Did it!"

Isaac Madie's eyes softened and the fingers of his hand moved. John reached for the fingers but could not get a hold. He lifted himself onto his elbows and dragged his bony, starved body the few feet to his father. Tears and sweat ran down his haggard face and pain tortured his body.

"Did it, Pa!" he said again.

Isaac Madie nodded. John grabbed his father's hand and worked his fingers up to the bulky wrist. His head dropped then and he lay panting, feeling the pain dying inside him. He didn't understand that either. In life he had understood very little and it was the same in death.

Isaac Madie's fingers folded over his son's hand and he muttered, "Boy, you proved to be the best of 'em. The best, boy."

John's face lifted and his eyes gleamed with joy. Then the big man's fingers curled open and his chest heaved one last time. John looked at his father and he could feel the night closing in. It struck him as strange that night should come so quickly. He held his father's hand firmly but gradually felt his own fingers losing their strength ...

Blake Durant had positioned himself between the hills and the buckboard. He was only fifty yards from Nyall when he saw him knocked to the ground. He watched in anger as John Madie rushed back to his father, only to be shot in the back by Ringo Nyall. Blake came off Sundown and hitched him in tight cover. Then he climbed to the top of a boulder and cupped his hands about his mouth.

"Nyall, listen to me!"

Ringo Nyall went down in a crouch beside the buckboard. Blake had a fair chance of hitting him from that distance but he was still worried about Angela Grant. Where was she?

"That you, Durant?" came Nyall's call a moment later.

"It is, Nyall. I've got you cut off. You can't go back because Sheriff Lasting and a posse of men from Glory Creek are coming from the north. You're trapped."

"The hell I am, Durant. I got the gold and I got the girl."

"You won't make it, mister."

"Who'll stop me? Now you draw back or by hell I'll put a slug in the woman right now."

Blake felt a surge of relief at knowing Angela was still alive. But Isaac Madie was most certainly dead. So was John Madie. That left him, Angela

Grant and Ringo Nyall, and Nyall held all the cards.

"Leave the gold and the girl," Blake said. "Do that and I'll let you ride out. Go while the going's good."

"The going ain't so bad from where L sit, Durant. You come closer and the girl gets it. Then you. I can match you mister, as easy as spittin'. I got them others and I'll get you, too!"

"You killed men who walked into death, Nyall. A kid could have done the same. But I'm a different proposition."

Nyall snorted angrily and crawled under the buckboard. Then he rose on the other side of the buckboard and stood against the warped timber, looking at the gold bars on the floor. He licked his lips. So close, so damned close.

"Durant, hear me now," he shouted. "I'm pulling out. I ain't wastin' time talkin' to you, not with them lawmen comin' up fast. You stay put, mister, right where you are. You fire at me or move at all, then Miss Grant gets it."

Blake wondered what chance he'd have if he charged Nyall now. But he decided that Nyall would carry out his threat to shoot the girl.

"You hear it, Durant? Follow and you get her killed. If you want her alive, you keep to hell off my heels. Past the hills I'll leave her trussed up where you can find her."

Getting no answer, Ringo Nyall climbed into the buckboard. He lifted Angela's unconscious body and pulled her beside him. He had to put an arm around her shoulder to keep her from falling, r Then he picked up the reins and hit the horses into a run. He worked the buckboard out of the clearing and sent it rocking along the main trail to the hills.

Behind him, Blake Durant wiped sweat from his face with his bandanna. Sundown stood quietly by, flicking flies away with his tail. Blake Durant, for one of the few times in his life, didn't know what to do.

Finally he led Sundown back to where the buckboard had stood. Then he walked to the bodies of Isaac Madie and his son, John. He knew with a glance that there was nothing he could do for them. He carried them into the shade and propped each against a tree. Then he swung onto Sundown. Having given Nyall ten minutes' start, he was going to dog the man to the edge of hell. He owed it to Angela Grant, and he owed it to the Madie family.

Sheriff Curly Lasting looked at the wide grave and frowned heavily. His men had checked out the clearing and discovered the tracks of the buckboard and a single horse, then tracks of two more horses.

Lasting said, "Looks to be two in there, and three went on after the buckboard. We were following five before."

None of the posse members spoke in return. The day's heat had taken the strength out of them. They looked worn and mean.

Curly Lasting looked ahead at the heat-seared country. Having put the desert behind them, he had intended to strike camp and give the men and the horses a breather. But with the evidence of people getting killed in this hell country, his own weariness dropped from him like water off shale. He said, "Okay, we're gaining on them, so we might as well keep the advantage. Ride as you like. If you get tired, drop out, then come on when you want. But keep comin', because we got forty thousand dollars' worth of bullion to get back and a killer to hang."

Curly Lasting hit his leg-weary horse into a run and led the way. When he looked back he was not surprised to find the townsmen following. They were a good bunch, he decided.

He rode through the noon heat and into the long afternoon. Coming to the clearing where Ringo Nyall had camped and left the buckboard,

Lasting stopped just short of the two men propped against a tree.

He recognized Isaac Madie and his son, John, and came wearily out of the saddle. His mouth was pinched tight and he had his own private thoughts about Isaac Madie now. But he kept them to himself. He directed a detail to bury, the dead and the others to rest up. But he didn't rest himself because there were too many disturbing thoughts in his head.

For one, the buckboard had been loaded with the bullion. The deeper tracks proved that. Also, one wheel was wobbling. That meant Nyall and the Grant woman could not proceed as fast as before. If they did, they would certainly come to grief on the way. And he knew that Nyall was driving for the horse behind had so even a stride that it had to be tethered short. The only other tracks were those of a single long-striding horse.

Durant's? Yes, Curly Lasting figured; Durant was still trailing Nyall. But since Madie and his sons had been killed, he couldn't work out what Durant was up to. Had he parted company with them? Had he in fact joined up with Nyall, and were they now partners? The more he thought about it, the more confused he became, and as soon as the burial party returned, he climbed back onto his horse. Four men immediately saddled up and came alongside him. But the others sat about watching him, waiting.

Lasting said, "I'm pushin' on. If you've read those buckboard tracks, you'll see that Nyall's loaded the gold bullion into it. So he won't be going on at any great rate now, and I think we'll catch sight of him before evening. Those who want to be in on the kill can ride with me. But nobody's pushing anybody. Some of you ain't young anymore and maybe all that enthusiasm you showed back in town has kinda dried up in you."

Lasting turned his horse and rode to the edge of the clearing. Then a smile broke across his mouth. He could hear the creak of saddle leather and the jingle of spurs. Within a few minutes the whole posse had formed up behind him. He said nothing as he rode into the heat.

TEN

BAPTISM OF FIRE

Blake Durant rode slowly, looking ahead. About him the terrain lay desolate, dead, bathed in burning sun glare. Nothing moved and now there was no wind. He thought of Isaac Madie and his four sons, all gone now. He thought, too about life and how strange it was, how a chance meeting with Isaac months ago had helped him to escape trouble with John, Mark and Luke Madie.

He'd gone to Glory Creek because he'd never come into this territory before. There had never been any time. The ranch and rearing his brother had taken up all his working moments and his spare time had been spent with Louise Yerby.

Blake touched the golden bandanna. She had given him the bandanna. Not a day without a thought of Louise, especially during the hours when he just drifted along, as he was doing now. Glory Creek had done nothing to erase her memory. Nor had the meeting with Isaac Madie and his boys; nor the meeting with Angela Grant.

He thought about Angela now, in the clutches of a killer. He remembered how pathetic she had looked in the rooming house foyer, a woman making a sacrifice of herself to get assistance for an ailing brother. He admired that in her, the unselfishness of the woman. But he remembered, too, the way she had looked at him, judging him as a man. He wondered if she studied other men in the same fashion.

He shrugged the thoughts away. He had to catch up with Nyall and either capture him or kill him. It didn't matter much either way.

He topped a rise and saw the buckboard ahead, close to the brooding hills and still going slowly. Ahead there was a break in the hills, a black mouthed passage which he knew led to the border country. Once through that gap, Nyall would be in territory where he could buy help from other hellions like himself.

Blake kept Sundown at an even pace, but the big black, showing no effects of the long tide across the barren country, kept straining for his head, as if he knew all this hardship would end only when Durant caught up with the buckboard. They travelled another two miles and Blake could see Nyall in the driving seat, his rifle propped against his thigh and Angela Grant seated with her back to Nyall. Blake checked the country ahead. He had no fears about taking on Nyall. He had met his kind before. But the girl presented a problem and he could see no way of solving it. As long as she was at Nyall's side, he would have to hold his fire for fear of killing her. So he had to trail in the hope that evening would come before Nyall reached a point of safety. Under cover of night, Blake felt he had a chance.

Another mile or so farther on, the buckboard swung towards the mouth of the passage. Blake was only three hundred yards to the rear of the buckboard, eating Nyall's dust, but out of range. He cursed when he saw the buckboard gather up a little speed and saw Nyall bringing a whip across the backs of the weary horses.

Blake spurted ahead, gun drawn. He drew himself upright in the saddle when he saw Angela suddenly jump from the buckboard and run, her hair and skirt flying wildly. Blake put Sundown to a run. Nyall had quickly whipped the buckboard about and was chasing Angela with it, working his rifle under his armpit as he went. Blake closed in. When he was about fifty yards from the buckboard, he opened fire.

His shots gained Nyall's attention and forced him to draw off from the chase. Blake kept going, his bullets splintering the sides of the buckboard. Nyall came about, drawing the horses to a dusty halt. He dropped into the back of the buckboard and Blake saw his rifle edge up. He swerved Sundown from one side to the other. His gun became empty and he hastily prodded fresh bullets from his gunbelt as he rode. Refilling the gun he kept swinging to the right and to the left, hearing Nyall curse him viciously.

Then he was only ten yards from the buckboard and Nyall was rising to his knees, the rifle at his shoulder. Blake dived from the saddle and let Sundown run on. He hit the ground ;on the point of one shoulder, rolled and came up with rifle slugs blasting the hard ground about him. Nyall stood above him, hate-filled eyes glaring down.

Blake's gun bucked in his hand. His bullet slammed into Nyall's shoulder and sent him reeling to the other side of the buckboard. He tripped over a bar of bullion and pitched to the ground. Blake fired under the buckboard's flooring and smashed the rifle from Nyall's hand. Nyall let out a howl, grabbed his torn wrist and looked anxiously about him, then he turned and broke into a run. Blake got to his feet, ran to the end of the buckboard and fired off two more shots.

Nyall was sent reeling by the first bullet and the second caught him behind his left knee. He went down near a boulder, then dragged himself forward as Blake triggered an empty gun.

Blake thrust cartridges into the cylinder. Angela Grant stood behind another rock watching him intently. He waved for her to take cover. When she bobbed from sight, he stepped into the open.

His movement brought a shot from Nyall. Blake's bullets gouged the rock face as he ran in a crouch. Then he leaned against a dead tree and refilled his gun. The fight was on, one he had not asked for. But it had come his way and there was no backing off.

He sleeved sweat from his face and dried his hands. Out in the clearing Sundown had stopped and was looking his way warily, legs quivering in indecision.

Blake waved him away.

Then he shouted, "You're hurt, Nyall. Throw out your gun!"

Nyall's answer was a bullet that ripped a slice of bark from the tree. Blake sighed. It would have to be to the death. The afternoon sun was burning on his skin, tightening the tension already in him. But inside he was completely cool. Nyall meant nothing to him now.

He walked from the cover of the tree and worked his way around the boulder. He held his gun at his waist, his hand rock-steady. His face was expressionless and not a nerve in his body moved. He walked on, his even-paced steps beating out sound from the hard ground. Nyall's head showed and then he stared in disbelief. He couldn't believe his good fortune. Durant must figure he was dead.

Nyall punched off a shot, but then a bullet took him squarely between the eyes, shutting off his cry of triumph. Blake Durant's calculated risk had paid off.

Nyall dropped onto the boulder and clawed his hands along its gritty surface. His gun slid from his fingers and he pitched down the side of the boulder, a jagged end of a rock catching at his cheekbone and slicing it open.

Blake walked to him, then holstered his gun. Suddenly he felt bone-weary.

Angela Grant watched the big man, Blake Durant, in the silence of pure astonishment. She found herself admiring him tremendously. No man had ever done for her what Durant had done. From the very beginning he had helped her He'd sent the Madie brothers packing, had escorted her through the town, had listened to her story and given her advice she now knew to be correct.

She set her teeth together hard. Nyall was dead. She had no doubt about that. Durant had shot him down mercilessly but she felt nothing. She had left her brother back in Cheyenne, and he was awaiting word from her. She had come into this hostile country to give herself to a man, to use his money to save her brother's life. But all that was finished with Nyall dead. There was no Zeb Ragnall. And there was no money, at least not for her.

Angela suddenly straightened. She watched Durant turn Nyall over with his boot and inspect the bullet holes. The buckboard horses had shifted down the clearing, away from the gunfire, and were now standing quiet. The passage to the border and hence to freedom was just before her, and Durant's horse was cropping grass at least a hundred yards from his master.

Angela gave a gasp at the simplicity of it all. Then she was running, going as fast as she could for the buckboard. She pulled herself up the side, sparing only one quick glance for the bullion loaded in the back and gleaming in the harsh sunlight. Angela felt excitement almost choking her. She picked up the reins and slashed them over the horses' backs. The animals lunged forward and Angela swung the buckboard in a circle and kept leathering them, driving them at all possible speed for the passageway. She saw Blake Durant draw back from Nyall, then turn, his gun leveling on her. But she didn't think for a moment that he would shoot at her.

Then she was into the passage opening and travelling through a dimness which frightened her. A long way ahead was the narrow corridor to freedom.

Blake clipped out an oath when he heard the buckboard moving off. He called to Sundown and the horse trotted over. He swung into the saddle and turned Sundown with a smooth pull on the reins. The big black lunged into a run and tore into the passage through the hills.

Within a mile Blake ran the buckboard down. Getting to the head of the lead horse, he grabbed the reins and drew back. Angela Grant reached for the driving whip. But the buckboard lurched to a halt and Blake walked Sundown back to her, catching the stock of the whip as she took it back to lash at him. He hurled the whip aside and said:

"Seems some of the bitterness has rubbed off on you, ma'am."

Angela glared, then a plea entered her eyes. "Please let me go, Mr. Durant. I need this gold."

"Take it and you'll end your days in jail," Blake said. "Too many people have been killed for it now, and the rightful owners don't care an owl hoot whether a thief is a man or a woman."

"Nobody knows who the rightful owners are, do they? Gold is just gold. It has no names stamped on it."

"It's bullion, pressed out in a certain way. And the rightful owner is the Wells Fargo Company, a powerful group who like a rake-off for their toil. You won't get away with it, Angela."

She just looked at him for a moment. "Would you really shoot me if I went on?"

Blake shrugged. "Don't reckon I would, ma'am."

"Then come with me. We can share it, marry, settle down. Nobody will ever know."

"I'll know."

Her stare went hard and her mouth tightened. She picked up the reins again. "I'll do it alone. I'm grateful for everything you've done for me, but I can't give all this up. Will you put the sheriff onto my trail?"

Blake pointed to the deep ruts in the ground behind the buckboard. "I won't have to. He can't be far behind now and he didn't strike me as a man who'd be sympathetic to a thief, woman or not. Sheriff Lasting is one of the old breed, teethed on honesty and fair play, but as hard as they come."

Angela looked towards the freedom only a few miles away. Blake edged Sundown closer.

"Six men have died over that gold and I want no part of it," Blake said. "But if you're so set on getting money, why not do it properly?"

Angela frowned at him. "How?"

"Turn back and give up the gold. The rest of your story will hold up, and then you'll collect the reward."

"Reward?" Excitement sparked in her blue eyes.

"The Wells Fargo Company always pays ten per cent reward for the return of stolen money. It's the way they have of getting honest people to work for them in rubbing out crime in these parts. Ten per cent of forty thousand dollars, Angela, is four thousand. That ought to set your brother up properly and leave something over for yourself."

"Four thousand dollars," she breathed.

Blake nodded and let Sundown turn away. But his look remained fixed on her. "Is that what you really want—to help your brother?"

Anger showed in Angela's face. "Of course it is!" she snapped. "How dare you suggest it might be otherwise?"

Blake gave her a wry smile. He pointed to the gold bullion scattered over the floor of the buckboard. "It's a lot of money."

He put Sundown into a walk and made his way back down the passage between the lava hills. But as he rode his ears were tuned for the sound of the buckboard moving again. When it came he concentrated hard, and when the sound became more distinct as the buckboard got closer, he smiled again.

He rode into the harsh sunlight and drew rein near the body of Ringo Nyall. Angela brought the buckboard beside him.

"What will we do with him?" she asked. "I—I can't look at him."

"We'll keep him," Blake said. "There's a price on his head."

Angela studied him grimly. He was like everybody else, she thought. For all his high and mighty ways, it came down to a matter of money finally. She watched him heft the body from the ground and lift it into the back of the buckboard.

A shudder ran through her at the thought of the dead man so close to her. Then Blake Durant led the way back across the open country and Angela let the tired horses walk in his wake.

It was an hour short of evening when Sheriff Curly Lasting showed up in the distance. Angela and Blake stopped the horses and Lasting came thundering on, his posse strung out in a line behind him. Drawing up beside the buckboard minutes later, Lasting looked keenly at Durant and then at Angela.

Blake said, "In the back, Sheriff."

Lasting's face registered surprise at the sight of the scattered bullion and Ringo Nyall's body. He swung back to face Durant.

"How'd it happen?"

Blake nodded towards Angela. "Miss Grant worked Nyall into a corner, then she called a warning to me and gave me the chance to gun him down. She wanted only to bring the bullion back and hand it over to the rightful owners."

Lasting's eyebrows rose in an arch. "That so, Miss Grant? Guess I owe you an apology. I figured you were in this mess up to your eye-teeth. Well, I was wrong, and I'm damn glad of it."

Lasting couldn't hide his relief and gratitude. As for Angela, she gave the lawman a shy smile and wondered what kind of a man he was. He was certainly handsome, she decided, and nicely built. And had a way of looking at her that suggested she appealed to him.

"Mr. Durant mentioned there was a reward for bringing the gold back," she said. "Is that true?"

"Damn tootin' it's true. And I'll see you get it, Miss Grant, every cent that's comin' your way." He swung on Durant again. "You claimin' for Nyall's carcass, Durant? Guess you got a right to."

Blake shook his head. "I'll make out without it, Lasting. Anything else you want with me?"

"Only some story-tellin', mister. All we done since we left Glory Creek was come on either graves or dead men. Five in all, counting Nyall there."

Blake removed his hat and refitted it to his head. "Miss Grant can tell you as much as I can, Sheriff, and she might be better at the telling than I am, since she was closer to the action most of the time. So, if you don't mind, I'll just drift. All right?"

Angela turned to face Blake. "You aren't coming back to Glory Creek, Mr. Durant?"

"The town doesn't hold much for me, ma'am. Might have in different circumstances, but that's not how it turned out."

Angela rose from the seat and smoothed down her skirt as Curly Lasting eyed her appreciatively.

She said, "If you don't mind, Sheriff, I'd like to talk to Mr. Durant in private."

Lasting nodded. "Just as you like, Miss Grant. I reckon that after what you've done out here, it ain't for me to tell you what to do or when."

Angela smiled. The sheriff would be easy to handle, she decided. She waited until the posse and Lasting had withdrawn before she turned to Durant. She looked directly into his eyes and said, quietly, "Do you have to go on, Blake? With the money we've got, we could make out real well."

Blake shook his head. "We're on .different trails, Angela. You want certain things and I want others."

"What do you want?" she asked.

His face clouded and his mouth tightened a little. He let his look sweep over her lush body and Angela felt no embarrassment. It was almost as if Durant had a right to look at her any way he pleased. She leaned forward, placed her hands on his shoulders and pulled his mouth towards hers. She lingered on the kiss, and his response sent waves of need through her. But when she drew back she saw that his face was expressionless.

"Who is she, Blake?" she asked softly.

But he moved Sundown back without a word. The black shifted impatiently under him, then

Blake gave a sudden dig of his knees that put Sundown into a run. Angela dropped back to the seat and picked up the reins. When Curly Lasting came to her, she said:

"I'm so exhausted, Sheriff. I don't think I can drive this buckboard another mile. Perhaps you could get one of the men to sit here and drive for me?"

Lasting licked at his lips and his eyes gleamed. "Why, hell, I should have thought of it myself. Sorry. Sule," he called to one of the posse members as he swung out of the saddle. A rider walked his horse forward. "Take 'em home, Sule. I'll see that Miss Durant gets back all right."

Sule Mitchener looked on curiously as Lasting hitched his mount to the buckboard, then turned his horse and shouted for the posse to pull out.

Angela shifted to make room for Lasting. When he was settled in beside her, she turned and watched the diminishing figure of Blake Durant atop his blue-black stallion. A sad look came into her eyes, but then she drew in her breath and smiled at Lasting.

"Are you married, Sheriff?"

Lasting shook his head. "Nope. I don't reckon I'm the kind that gets hogtied to a woman's apron. I need plenty of room to move, plenty of time to make my own decisions. I don't like bein' badgered and told what to do."

Angela worked a hand under his forearm and leaned closer. Lasting frowned, conscious of the softness of her body against him.

"Take it slowly, please, Sheriff. I'm so worn out."

"Sure, sure," he said. "I'll walk 'em real slow."

Angela nestled against him and thought of Ringo Nyall and Blake Durant. Then she erased them from her mind completely and concentrated on Curly Lasting, unmarried and with a responsible job.

He'd make a good husband, she decided.